CRASH AND BURN

REBEL RACERS BOOK 3

SUSAN HARRIS

CRASH AND BURN
Copyright ©2022 Susan Harris
All rights reserved.

Originally published as Kindle Vella Episodes

ISBN: **978-1-63422-525-0** (paperback)
Cover Design by: Gem Promotions
Typography by: Gem Promotions

PROLOGUE

Luke

LUKE HADN'T BEEN able to swallow down his anger after his near miss yesterday but he closed his eyes to get focused as he took his spot on the grid and the rain continued to pelt down on them.

"Radio check, one, two."

"Loud and clear, mate," Luke replied to his race manager, flexing his fingers as he put down his visor as the red lights flashed overhead and then went out and Luke floored it, slipping down the inside and making up two places when the front two cars were slow off the mark.

The rain came down heavier, affecting their visibility, and Luke was surprised that no one had spun off or taken each other out. Luke had no grip and it was only years of practice during winter rain and sleet that meant he had the upper hand.

His race manager told him that a few drivers at the back of the pack had slid off and were making their way back onto the track with caution.

Luke knew that this was his best chance at getting a podium place, and being an F1 driver was all about taking chances so he went as fast as he dared with the way the weather was until he'd lapped the back markers and came up to the idiot who had almost caused him to crash yesterday.

"Fucking asshole," Luke muttered to himself, forgetting that everyone would hear him as the blue lights flashed to remind the idiot to let Luke pass him. But the dickhead didn't slow and didn't let him by.

"Unbelievable."

Luke had no choice but to force his way past, speeding up to overtake him so that the idiot's stupid behaviour wouldn't ruin his race.

As a formula one driver, Luke had seen his fair amount of crashes. He'd had a crash or two himself and knew it came with the job, part of the risks involved in the industry.

But when he woke that morning, he'd never seen this coming.

Luke was trying to lap the car in front when it swerved in Luke's direction and clipped the back of his wheel. Luke's tyre blew, causing his car to weave on the track as he tried to regain control, cursing as the bloody fool came at Luke again, leaving Luke powerless to stop the impact.

His body was thrown around like a ragdoll despite the cage, as the car flipped, rolling over and over, Luke's body rippling with pain as the car tried to eject him, and yet, even with the halo protecting his head, his body felt like it was shattering from the inside. The car crumpled around him, hitting the barrier finally, upside down with Luke hanging inside the car.

Luke barely heard his race manager ask if he was okay, but couldn't answer him, because his body began to shut down like a broken machine, and all he could think before darkness consumed him was that he didn't want to die.

Chapter One

Luke

Five Months Later

Luke could vaguely make sense of the conversations that were happening around him, of the medical terms being thrown around but he didn't know how much of it was real and how much of it was just his mind playing tricks on him. He heard the voices of those he loved, his parents, his best friends Noah and Quinn, but most of all, he heard the voice of his twin, and that pierced through the amount of drugs in his system to keep him under.

Luna was the other part of him. Luke could read her moods as if they were his own and she was the same. When they were babies, according to their mother,

5

neither of them would sleep unless the other one was within reaching distance. When Luna wailed, the moment Luke would reach out for her, she'd instantly calm down.

They were like yin and yang. Luna was loud and he was quieter. Luna was spontaneous while Luke was more pragmatic liking plans and preparation. Luna was fearless and Luke, well, despite his calm, smiling exterior, was a symphony of fear.

But Luke was not scared of dying ...

No...he was terrified that unlike his rockstar sister, he would fail and let everyone down. If he woke up from his injuries, he was scared that the one thing that he was good at, the one thing that was his and his alone, would be taken from him.

Luke felt Luna brush the strands of his hair away from his face and he wished he could lean into her touch, to let his older sister reassure him that after this, he wouldn't be any more broken than he already was.

Pain seared him at the waist. It had been coming more and more over the last few days, and Luke felt more aware of his surroundings. He heard his mother's knitting needles to his right, he heard the faint snores from his father as they rumbled somewhere in the room. He could hear his sister shouting encouraging words at the TV.

A pang smashed into his chest as he made out the achingly familiar sounds of cars racing on a track. He listened to the cheers, to the roar of the crowd, and it was like he was back inside his race car, feeling the exhilaration of driving at breakneck speeds and depending on his skills to keep the car from crashing and push for the win.

It was the one thing that he was good at. If he lost that...what else would he be?

He kept so much of himself hidden; his fears, his anxieties, his sexuality, all because of this unwavering dream of being a world champion F1 driver. He told himself time and time again that it was worth it to achieve his dreams. All of it was worth it. The training, the diet, the continuous travel to every side of the globe to race but never truly visiting a country.

He'd committed himself to spending his life alone because he wanted to be judged on the merits of his driving and not the fact that he was a gay man in a sport that to his knowledge, had not had one before.

White hot agony speared him again at the waist and Luke was suddenly aware of blaring alarms, his parents' shouts of concern, and then, things began to sharpen. The voices of the doctors became clearer, the sounds of the hospital he was obviously in became almost irritating to his ears, and the overwhelming scent of disinfectant was unbearable.

Awareness tugged on his senses, as accents that were obviously not Irish said his name.

His throat burned like he had downed an entire bottle of tequila.

"Luke, can you hear me?"

"Yes." He tried to reply but the grogginess hadn't fully cleared.

"Luke, it's time to open your eyes. There's a lot of people here eager to see you awake."

Luke peeled open his eyes and the first thing he noticed was the whiteness of the ceiling as a dark-skinned doctor grinned at him with a big smile and bright white teeth.

"Ah good. Welcome back, Luke."

He tried to say something, even groan at the intense pain in his body, but it felt as if there was something preventing. Luke lifted his arm, noting how much effort it took, and reached to touch his mouth and found a tube there. Panic welled inside his chest as he pawed at the tube but his hands were gently taken away.

"Luke, there's a tube in your throat that helped you breathe while you were sleeping but we'll remove it now. Can you blink once if you understand me?"

He blinked once in response, felt himself want to go back to sleep. There was a nauseating feeling as they removed the tube and Luke coughed, the sound a wheezing and harsh as he gagged and it made him want to puke. A nurse gave him a sip of water, and it tasted like the most delicious thing he'd ever drank.

Luke must have dozed off again, because the next time he woke there was a doctor listening to the rapid beating of his heart.

"G'day mate, it's good to have you back with us. How you feeling?"

Luke swallowed hard, winced at the pain but managed to get a word out. "Sore."

"That's to be expected. You gave a lot of people a scare. I'm going to ask you a few questions and then once we've got all the procedures out of the way, you can see your family."

Luke answered the questions as best he could, the only stumbling block was when the doctor asked him if he knew the date and Luke shook his head. Then Luke glanced down and saw the way his hips and legs were pinned to the bed and he started to panic.

It must have shown in his eyes because the doctor asked him to look at him and Luke did.

"I'm not going to sugarcoat it for you, Luke. You've been in a medically induced coma for the last couple of months. You had a very serious crash that almost killed you but you fought your ass off to stay alive. Your broken pelvis has healed nicely and after physiotherapy, we are confident that you will walk again."

Glancing down at the scary contraption holding his legs in place, Luke wasn't sure he shared the doctor's optimism and it must have shown because the doctor smiled. "I know it doesn't seem it now, but a couple of months and you'll be back on your feet."

Luke wasn't really all that concerned about getting

on his feet. The way his legs felt like lead was the least of his problems.

"How long?" Luke found himself asking, his voice sounding hoarse from not using it.

"How long for what?" the doctor asked, but from the expression, Luke knew that he understood what Luke was asking.

"How long until I get back in my car? When can I race again?"

The doctor frowned, straightening as he held Luke's gaze and from the look in the man's eyes, Luke could tell it was gonna be bad. The machine that was connected to his heart started to beep rapidly in time with his increasing heart rate.

Luke tried to brace himself for what was next to come out of the doctor's mouth but nothing could prepare him. It was like being tossed around again in the car as it rolled over and over, flinging him about.

"Luke, I'm going to be honest with you, okay? You have a long road to recovery. But, you need to prepare yourself that you may never be as fit as you were. That means, there is a strong chance that you never drive in formula one again."

No...just fucking hell no....

"You're wrong. You're fucking dead wrong." Luke ripped the chords attached to his chest and tossed them aside, ignoring the blaring from the machines. He reached down and unsuccessfully tried to yank his legs free of the binds. He snarled in frustration and shoved away at the doctor's hands when he tried to stop him.

Luke heard the doctor call for a nurse as he held Luke's arms while Luke continued to struggle against his grasp, trying to buck off the hold. He suddenly felt all drowsy, and his limbs felt like noodles.

They were wrong. He'd prove them all fucking wrong and he'd get back in his car and prove it!

He had to.

His eyes grew heavy and Luke was powerless to stop his mind from plunging back into the murky depths of darkness.

CHAPTER TWO

Luke

ONE MONTH Later

Luke stared blindly around the facility as the nurse wheeled his chair around the state-of-the-art gym and rehabilitation centre. The last four weeks had shaken Luke to his core. The first time he had gotten out to stand, still in the hospital in Australia, he'd been so weak that two nurses had to lunge for him when he couldn't even support himself with the walking frame.

His lack of progress had soured his mood. He'd pushed away everyone in his family to the extent that he had told doctors he refused to see anyone until he was back to normal. His parents had returned to Ireland at his request, and it had taken a very heated argument with Luna before his twin had left him alone too.

"Luke, c'mon. Mam is in tears because you sent her away. She doesn't want to leave you alone in a foreign country like this."

"Like what, Luna? A fucking cripple? Because that's what I am. She doesn't need to see that."

Luna swept her ruby red hair off her face, her eyes soft and it irritated Luke. "You're not a cripple, Luke. We just all want to see you home. Shutting out your family, your friends, won't do you any good."

Luke felt anger, white-hot and burning under his skin. "Fuck off, Luna. Fuck off back to your perfect life and leave me alone. I don't need you to boss me around anymore. And you can tell Noah and Quinn and everyone else that I don't want to see them. I just want to be left alone."

There had been a few more words thrown that he wasn't proud of but in the end, it was Charlotte Coyle who had shown up to the hospital in Australia and laid out what was going to happen now.

"Rebel Racers wants to ensure the recouperation from the crash is as seamless as possible. The doctors here have cleared you to fly home to Cork, where you will attend a very private sports injury clinic." Charlie had told him. Her eyes had been kind, even if her face was in business mode.

Luke hadn't had the energy to argue with Charlie, not even when Charlie had rested her hand on Luke's.

"I know you're hurting right now, but Noah and Quinn really need to see you."

"And I need my legs to work so I can get back in my car. From all the news reports, they managed perfectly fine without me for the last six months."

He knew full well he was being an asshole, however, it hurt him that life had continued while he was laying on his ass. Noah and Charlie had gotten engaged, Quinn and her racer manager had hooked up and were living together. He couldn't help the bitterness that swirled in his veins that while he was unconscious, bones broken, his friends and family had moved on with their lives.

Luke had just come back from physical therapy, frustrated and tired, and very anger at himself and his body and someone had left the TV on. There was a highlight show that was replaying the best bits of the first half of the season and the presenters started showing a highlight reel of Quinn's best performances since getting in the car.

As Luke watched Quinn take the podium in France next to Noah, their smiles radiant and bright, it had awakened a dark and twisted part of him that he couldn't shove back down. He knew he should be happy for the girl he thought of as another sister, but she was in his seat because some dickhead crashed into him.

He started to see Quinn as much of an obstacle as his stupid legs to getting back in the car and even after his phone had been returned to him, he had left any messages unread.

Why did this have to happen to him? How could everyone around him be happy and get everything they wanted? All he had was his ability to drive. He couldn't or rather felt he couldn't go public with his sexuality because it would become the media's main focus and then it would be less about his driving ability and more about who he might be hooking up with.

"Luke, do you want to see your room?" Penelope asked him, his new personal nurse and aid as she pushed him along the halls and Luke just shrugged. He hadn't said much since getting off the flight from Oz and being chauffeured to this very exclusive and private rehab clinic that had several high profile sports clients.

His personal bedroom was more like a hotel suite, with bay windows overlooking the city. It had a bedroom area and a lounge area with a wheelchair accessible bathroom. His room had all the mod cons and it reminded him of the time he and Noah, after their rookie F2 season, went to Spain and rented a villa. Each room had their own apartment and Noah, who had lived in care most of his life, hadn't know what to do with a fancy place like that so they ended up sleeping on the floor outside by the pool.

"Well, this is home sweet home for the next couple of months," Penelope said cheerfully, wheeling Luke to the window where he could look outside. "You want me to call anyone now you've gotten settled? I'm sure your family would love to see you. Or maybe you want to get freshened up?"

His lack of personal hygiene was the last thing on his mind, but maybe Penelope had a point. Glancing at his reflection in the glass as rain began to fall outside, Luke didn't recognise the person staring back at him. His ginger hair was shaggy and disheveled, his eyes had dark circles around them and the stubble he usually kept trimmed on his face, now looked as bad as his hair.

"I'm fine." He grunted out, drawing a sigh from Penelope, who proceeded to walk around the room and tell him where things were, how the bed worked, and how to call for a nurse if he needed one. Luke had gotten pretty good in the short space of four weeks with his upper body strength so he could move from his bed to the chair and back again.

It was the lack of power in his legs that kept him awake at night with cramps and restlessness. It was the nightmares of the crash replaying over and over in his mind that startled him awake, and it was his screams that filled the emptiness of the night when he was certain that he'd died and was reliving his death on a loop.

"Well, that's the grand tour done for now. You eat and get some rest. Tomorrow is gonna be a long day. You have a couple of sessions planned, one with the psychologist, and then your new personal trainer wants to asses to see how much improvement you've made in the last couple of weeks."

"He's gonna be seriously disappointed because it's been fuck all." He drawled and Penelope laughed.

"Don't be so hard on yourself, Luke. It will all work out how it's meant in the end. Now, before I cosy up with a boxset and some wine, what can I get you to eat? Has to be something you're craving after all that Aussie food."

Normally he would have told Penelope that he wasn't hungry or ordered something that his nutritionist had planned into his strict diet, but if he was being technical about it, it was the summer break when he normally took time off and ate what he wanted and drank before getting back into shape.

He was about to tell Penelope that he wasn't hungry when his stomach rebelled against him and rumbled, making Penelope lift her brows.

"I suppose chips and curry and a burger are out of the question?" He asked sheepishly.

Penelope winked at him, smiling. "Nope! There have to be benefits of being stuck in this snazzy posh place. Let me send someone out for Lennox's. If that's what you fancy."

Luke thanked her, then the woman left to sort out the food and he wheeled his chair away from the window and picked up his phone, seeing a tirade of messages that were still left unread. He felt a little bit guilty that he hadn't made the effort to contact Noah or Quinn, but he couldn't stand to see them and have them look at him with pitiful eyes.

The doctors in Australia had told him that they were just as worried about his mental health as his physical health but Luke had dismissed them. They worried that his state of mind would hamper his recovery, hence the appointments with the psychologist. No doubt they had reported to Charlie as CEO of Rebel Racers that they were concerned.

So, Luke knew he needed to get better at faking it and if Luke was still good at anything, he was good at putting on a fake smile and pretending to be something other than his true self.

CHAPTER THREE

Emil

EMIL HAD LANDED in Ireland last night and after dinner in the hotel restaurant, he and his crutches went to bed before checking into his fancy new rehab centre the next day in order to get himself back fighting fit after he tore a ligament during a soccer match last week. He had intended to make full use of the training facility in Denmark to rehab, but then his best friend had told him about this state of the art facility so he had decided to spend some time in Ireland.

Oskar had been his best friend since the day Oskar had shared his lunch with Emil, and they had remained as close as brothers through many ups and downs,

Oskar's mother Alma becoming like a second mother to him. Emil had loving parents, but they could not afford the three children they had, so Emil had worked weekends on a fishing boat when his father lost the use of his hand, even as he tried to hone his football skills.

When he was spotted by a scout at fifteen, he had been able to change his family's life. He had signed deals with sponsors and purchased a house for his parents to raise his little sisters comfortably. He wasn't one of those young footballers who splurged on expensive cars and homes. Emil had invested his money wisely, so that even if football was to end tomorrow, he would never again be the boy in the schoolyard with no lunch.

When Oskar had taken the job at Rebel Racers, an Irish-owned Formula 1 team, Emil had been sad to see his friend leave the Danish team, but happy that Oskar was finally trying to step out of the shadows of his dickhead dad. Viggo wanted his son to be just like him; a materialistic man who was chasing his youth with women who were decades younger than him.

But Oskar was nothing like his father and had his mother's upbringing to thank for that. Now, Oskar was happily dating his girl racer and Emil was thrilled to see him so enamoured by the young woman. Quinn was a fighter, a survivor, one who did not give affection easily and yet, Emil could see just how well they fit together on the numerous times over the past few months they had been in the same room.

It reminded him of the conversation he had with Oskar, having just met Quinn for the first time and how he had helped nudge Oskar in the right direction.

"You like her."

Emil waited until Oskar had sat back down and answered with a yes then didn't elaborate, which was the way with his brother. Emil ordered more drinks, waiting until they arrived before he took a drink from his bottle, leaning back in his chair as he set his drink down and folded his arms across his chest.

"You have that face you get when you are being too serious. It will give you wrinkles my handsome friend." Emil teased Oskar, loved it when the far too serious man threw back a sarcastic comment of his own.

It had taken Emil months to get the boy to laugh, months before he had relaxed enough to get up to mischief with Emil. It was only when the two of them had been playing in Oskar's home and his father had frowned at the sound of the boys' laughter that Emil had understood why Oskar did not laugh so freely.

"As you like to point out to me whenever you get the chance, I am always too serious."

They held each other's gaze for a few minutes then Emil said. "In the past, you have dated women who were smart, attractive, academic, and not at all suited to you. It's your safety net, Oskar. Because deep down, you know that you would never be content with someone like that and it prevents you from having your heart involved."

"I did not know that you had been studying psychology, Emil."

Tone as icy and calm as ever, that sharpness had never bothered Emil "I know you as well as you know me. You may have always been serious, yet, you throw yourself out of planes to feel that rush. A normal woman would not be the right match for you. You deserve someone who challenges you, who argues with you, who makes you want to be less serious. Tell me, Oskar, what is holding you back this time?"

Oskar gave Emil the responsible, respectable answer to explain his reluctance to exploring the connection he had with the racer. "We are just starting to work together. It would be inappropriate for me to engage in something like this."

"Like this?" Emil laughed, taking another sip of his beer. "You make it sound like you are filling in tax forms. You cannot help how you feel, Oskar. But I do not think that is the reason. I think you are afraid."

Oskar froze midway through taking a sip from his bottle and put his beer back down on the table. "Afraid?"

"Yes," Emil felt himself grow angry at his friend, knowing that he himself was afraid to be himself, especially with Oskar. "You are afraid that if you allow yourself to have feelings for Quinn, that you may become your parents. In one way, you are terrified that you would hurt Quinn like your father hurt your mother. In another way, you are afraid of becoming like Alma, trapped inside your mind and forcing someone

you love to watch you become unlike the person you once were."

A flash of emotion flared in Oskar's eyes as he said. "It is not as simple as that, Emil. It isn't."

Emil sighed, frustrated that he was projecting his own feelings onto Oskar, but Emil knew his friend well enough to know that with Oskar, sometimes, you needed to give him a little push in the right direction. "It could be. You confuse people, Oskar. Those who do not know you think you lack emotions, but I know that when you are angry, your tone becomes so cold I feel a chill. You let people think you are indifferent because it protects you from letting people in. Life is passing you by and you spend your time jumping out of planes, rock climbing and all that because it is a safe way to feel exhilaration."

Oskar stared at him, not responding so Emil continued. "You could never be Viggo, Oskar. You have the kindest heart I know. You deserve to be free of the shackles of your parents and live your own life. And, knowing Alma, I think she would like your Quinn."

It made his heart hurt to think of Oskar's mother, the kindest, most caring person he knew besides his own mother who on his last visit, only recalled him as a young boy and Emil had played along. He had not told Oskar just how much his mother had declined.

"If the prospect of losing your memories is what holds you back from seeing if this thing with Quinn is real, then do the goddamn test and stop hiding behind a monster that might not be under the bed."

Thankfully, Oskar had taken his advice and now, his friend was happier than he ever had been. The change in his demeanour wouldn't be noticeable to most, but Emil had seen it, the relaxed stance, the way he smiled at Quinn when he thought no one was looking. And Quinn, the woman who was guarded and rightly so, her face softened when she was with Oskar.

And by the gods, Emil was jealous that he had no one to look at him like Quinn and Oskar looked at one another. It made him ache to have what his friend had. Someone to come home to every night. Someone to know all the parts of you and accept them.

Emil was devoted to his sport, devoted to his family and friends, and while he had some relationships with women and men, he just hadn't truly told anyone about his sexuality, and that made him close himself off to the possibility of a meaningful relationship.

He was terribly lonely despite being surrounded constantly by people, but he wanted more from life than just being the top scoring Danish international footballer.

Maybe the break in Ireland would do him the world of good, and when he and Oskar came face to face in a few weeks, perhaps Emil could start by telling Oskar how he had been feeling lately.

As if Emil had summoned him, his phone rang and he smiled as he answered. "Oskar."

Emil listened as Oskar spoke, his smile faltering,

but by the end of the conversation, when Oskar told him that he needed his help, Emil could only agree with his friend and promised to do what he could.

Looks like Emil had a date with an injured, stubborn F1 driver.

CHAPTER FOUR

Luke

LUKE GRITTED his teeth and swallowed down the groan of pain as his legs screamed at him as he white-knuckled the bars and tried to make his legs move how he wanted them to. It was his fifth time walking the length of the parallel bars. His physio was telling him just how good he was doing, especially given the fact six weeks ago, Luke had been in a medically induced coma.

But Luke was frustrated at the slow progress especially after his parents had shown up yesterday and fussed over him. Luke had wanted to send them away, not wanting anyone to see him like this, but his mother had looked like she was about to cry and Luke hadn't the heart to fight her.

Instead he had pretended he was okay, faked a smile, and even managed a laugh as his mother filled him in on all the news that he had missed, not realizing that the very fact that Luke had missed so much caused him pain. However, Luke had drank his tea, ate the Madeira cake his mother had baked, and listened as his mother told him all about Luna's bands' record deal, Noah and Charlie's engagement, and Quinn's new romance. His mother told him about how Noah and Declan had been helping around the bar when they had been in Australia.

None of them broached anything F1-related, even though Luke knew the drivers had just returned from their summer break and had a race this weekend. If his timing was right and no changes had been made to the race calendar while he was unconscious, the team would be at the Dutch Grand Prix this weekend. Noah and Quinn had tried to come see him during their downtime, but Luke had sent them away.

If he was being honest with himself, it was really Quinn he couldn't look at. She had his seat and she was outperforming him. It....hurt him. Back in Oz, he had turned on the TV and accidentally turned on a sports channel where they were highlighting Quinn's road to success. It outlined her podiums, her aggressive driving style, and how she was an inspiration for female drivers. Luke had been about to turn it off, the pain in his chest like a ton weight when the report went to a question Quinn was asked after the French Grand Prix after her podium place.

"Quinn, how will the team decide on who keeps the seat if Luke Sullivan wakes up?"

Quinn lifted her head and glared. "When...when Luke wakes up."

The reporter smiled as Quinn shrugged her shoulders. "Listen, when that happens, I will do what the team wants and what they decide. I am aware that my seat has a time limit and for now, I'm just focused on getting as many points as possible for the team and doing all I can to help Noah, who has a fighting chance for the championship."

"But with you driving up a storm right now, do you think the team will have a tough decision ahead to pick their second driver?"

Quinn's eyes darkened, as she sat back in her seat. "I can't predict the future. So stop asking me stupid questions and stop trying to stir crap that isn't relevant."

Luke had switched off the TV, feeling a little sad at the way he had ghosted his best friends but he didn't want to see the pity in their eyes. And because the question that the reporter had asked was a valid question, how would the team decide on who got to drive the car, especially when Quinn was absolutely killing it at the moment? He had always known that Quinn was a formidable force in a car and he and Noah had even wondered if she would get tired of waiting for her shot and leave them for another team.

Now, she didn't have to …

Pain shot through his hip and Luke barked out a curse, thankful that he was the only one in the state-of-the-art gym this morning. His knees threatened to buckle but Luke managed to make it to the end of the walk.

"Good Luke. I think that's enough for this morning. We can work out some more in the pool this afternoon."

"Just one more length. I can do it."

"Luke …you're pushing too much. You need time to recover and I know that you are in pain."

Luke ignored his physio, Mark, turned himself around and began the agonising walk again. Of course, he was in pain, of course, he was pushing. He was a Twenty-three-year-old race car driver on the brink of losing the one thing that he was good at, the one thing that was his. If he lost the ability to be a racer, then who the hell was he?

The muscles in his thighs screamed at him, the blood pounding as he missed a step, and would have face-planted had he not grabbed onto the bars with an iron grip. His arms burned as Mark rushed forward and made to help him back to his feet.

"Don't." Luke snarled at the physio, fighting against the pain to right himself. Luke closed his eyes, willing himself to take another step, to push harder, to push more and he did, his body trembling as he took another step then another, reaching the end of the walk and he knew, deep down, he wasn't going to make the return journey back again and not do himself more harm than good.

Luke managed to get himself into his chair, releasing a breath as the relief surged through him once he took the weight off his feet. He felt drained and knew he'd probably drop off to sleep before lunch and before he was scheduled to have a workout in the pool.

He had never been much of a swimmer, but over the last month or so, when he started his rehabilitation, getting in the pool was the freest he had felt since he had woken up. His legs moved mostly with no pain while he was in the pool, and despite the grumbling he did, Luke was enjoying the time spent in there.

A throat cleared off to the side and Luke's eyes flung open. Standing in the doorway, balanced on crutches, was the most beautiful man Luke had seen in his life. Dark brown eyes looked at him, dark hair and stubble framing a striking face, and lips that looked like they could kiss a fire along his skin. His skin had a faint golden glow and his body, damn, even through the tight t-shirt and shorts, Luke could see the chorded muscles.

And he knew who the man was. Emil Anderson, Danish soccer superstar. Luke was a soccer fan, knew just how good Emil was on the pitch, and had always known he was handsome. But in person, the man was absolutely devastating.

Desire flooded through Luke and heat flushed his cheeks.

"I am sorry to intrude but I was told it was okay to work out here?"

Mark walked over and introduced himself to Emil, but Luke could feel Emil watching him.

"If you need any help with your rehab, I'm more than happy to help."

"I suppose a blowjob is out of the question?" Luke muttered under his breath and his cheeks heated even more, but it looked like Emil hadn't heard him as he came towards Luke and when Emil smiled, Luke felt his heart race and he told himself it was just because Luke was meeting another famous sportsman.

The Danish man smiled as he balanced on his crutches and held out his hand. "Emil Anderson. You must be the infamous Luke Sullivan I've heard so much about."

For a moment, Luke was puzzled how the footballer would have heard so much about him, and then his mind caught up that Emil and Oskar, Quinn's boyfriend, were friends.

Annoyance plucked at the strings of his temper as Luke ignored Emil's outstretched hand and steered himself toward the exit. "Have you been sent to spy on me?"

Emil chuckled, running a hand through his hair.

"Of course. I tore ligaments in my knee just so I could spend a few months on the sidelines, not playing the game I love, just to spy on you."

Luke glared at him but Emil firmly held his ground. "But since I am here, and you and I are the only two VIPs residing on the third floor, I was hoping we could outlast the boredom and spend some time together."

Luke snorted, shaking his head. "I don't need a pity friend. And I don't need you running back to Quinn and telling her how badly I'm progressing. So, thanks but no thanks."

Leaving the footballer behind, Luke wheeled himself out of the room without looking behind him, even though every instinct in him was begging him to glance over his shoulder and take one last look at the gorgeous man.

CHAPTER FIVE

Emil

"I suppose a blowjob is out of the question?"

It had taken Emil's best poker face not to react when Luke had muttered the quip, the red-haired driver's cheeks flushing as he had checked to see if Emil had heard him, looking almost relieved when Emil made no indication that he had.

When Emil had spoken to Oskar a few days ago, telling him all about Luke and how everyone was worried about him, Oskar had not told him anything about Luke's personal life and now Emil expected it was because the racer was very much in the closet.

And Emil had to admit that part intrigued him more than it should. Reddish blond hair and vivid green eyes, freckles adorned his cheeks, and a faint ginger beard that was more pronounced in the sunlight, Emil liked what he saw but he knew it was wholly inappropriate to be perving on the man who was dealing with so much.

Luke had fled the gym, stating that he had known that Emil was here as a spy, and he wasn't looking for a pity friend, but Emil knew that Luke was fighting a wave of depression about his injuries. He had seen many a footballer in a similar state after an injury. He himself had been lucky that it was just ligament damage and he knew he would be back on the pitch in no time.

After his session, Emil had a quiet lunch in his room, which happened to be right across the hall from Luke's, and while Emil had his doors and blinds open, Luke's were shut. Emil had caught a glimpse of the driver on his return from swimming, after being wheeled in by an older woman who managed to drag a bark of laughter from Luke.

Emil had gone for another session in the afternoon, with his own physio telling him that he could probably lose the crutches in a few days. Emil was thrilled to hear that, although he was forbidden from putting his feet on a ball for another couple of weeks.

The rooms to the front of the rehabilitation centre all had doors that led out to an adjoining balcony. Tonight, the rain was falling down in torrents, the sound beating against the roof, and Emil found it hard to sleep. He was a social creature who despised spending time alone because it gave him too much time to think.

Emil left his crutches to the side and made his way outside, inhaling the scent of the rain as he sank down on one of the chairs that was under a slatted roof. His skin was pimpled from the chill but he was a Dane and the Danes knew this was not cold. He and Oskar had faced harsh winters in Denmark, the walk to school in winter a workout in itself.

Lightning streaked across the sky and Emil was struck by just how beautiful the sky looked, the streak of blazing light across a pitch black sky. Emil felt the restlessness in him relax and he was about to make his way back inside to see if he could sleep when he heard the furthest door over open and watched as Luke wheeled himself out.

The other man obviously didn't notice Emil out on the balcony, and Emil didn't know how he could slip inside without Luke noticing him leave. Luke moved toward the stone wall and leaned his elbows on the ledge, then held out his hand as if he wanted to capture the rain in his grasp.

Under the yellow glow of the moonlight, Emil could see the expression on Luke's face, a look of utter sadness that made Emil want to hug the other man and it surprised him how insane the urge was.

Instead, Emil decided he had to let Luke know that

he was not alone on the roof so as not to startle the other man when he realized the same thing.

"I bet it's nice to see the rain after being stuck in Australia since you woke up."

Luke's head jerked around, his eyes wide and Emil watched as Luke's eyes quickly scanned over him. Emil got up off his seat and made his way over to where Luke was and pulled a chair over so they were seated at the same level.

"The last time I heard the rain like this was the night before the crash," Luke said quietly, turning his head to look at Emil. "I didn't think the sound of rain could trigger nightmares but here I am."

Luke looked sheepish after making the admission to Emil and Emil wanted to reassure him that he was not the only one who was triggered by silly things.

"I remember for the longest time after my father's accident, the sound of the waves used to fill my stomach with dread. Even when I was on the fishing boat myself, it made me feel queasy."

Luke's lips quirked into a tight smile. "What happened to your dad?"

"He got tangled up in a net when out to see fishing and it pulled him under the water. The net cut off the circulation to his wrist with the way it entangled him. We were lucky he did not drown."

Luke was quiet for a few minutes as he seemed to mull over what Emil had said and when he did speak, he seemed to have lost some of the tension that had been weighing down his body.

"When I woke in Oz, I was desperate to come home and start to get back to normal, but now that I'm home, well, stuck here, I can't seem to settle. I thought the familiarity would push me to work harder but I feel like I'm suffocating."

Emil understood what Luke was saying and perhaps that was the reason why he had jumped at the chance to rehab in Ireland and not back home in Denmark, where his family would have smothered him with love and his team would have been watching to see his progress to make sure their star striker was fit and ready for world cup qualifiers.

"Sometimes, it's better to have the reassurance of the familiar when the world is uncertain. I'm sure that once you settle in, you will start to feel more yourself."

Luke glanced at Emil again and sighed. "I guess you'll report back and tell them all that I'm struggling now, right?"

Emil ran his hand through his hair. "I admit to being asked to make sure that you were okay as we would both be here. But anything you tell me stays with me. I know that there are a lot of people who love you and want to make sure you know you are not alone. If I say anything, it will be that you are coping remarkably well for someone who survived what you did."

This time, when Luke flashed him a smile, Emil felt something knot inside him.

"I appreciate that. And I'm sorry for being an asshole. I promise I'm not always like that."

Emil knew Luke wasn't normally like this. When he had returned to his room for dinner, Emil had nosed on Luke's socials and the smiling, happy man in the photos seemed a world away from the somewhat defeated man sitting beside him.

"I meant what I said when I offered to keep you company if you a wanted. But only if you promise not to be my pity friend."

Luke barked out a laugh and angled his chair so that he was looking at Emil. "You're gonna throw that at me whenever the opportunity arrives, aren't ya?"

"It's what pity friends are for," Emil remarked with a wink and a smile as Luke's cheeks flushed.

They sat in silence for a while, the rain falling down, until Luke yawned, covering his mouth to try and suppress it. Emil chuckled and slowly got to his feet. "Well, since I have bored you to sleep, I think it might be a good time to head to bed."

Luke blinked, his mouth opening as if he was shocked at the implication and Emil was enjoying shocking the racer out of his depressed state even if the other man had no idea that Emil not only liked men but had suspected that Luke also liked men.

"Perhaps we can have dinner together tomorrow

and we can chat some more," Emil said as he walked toward his door.

"Sure, okay…" Luke answered as he wheeled himself back to his own door.

"Goodnight, Luke," Emil said before ducking back inside his room as he heard Luke say goodnight to him before he went back into his room and closed the door.

Even though it was really late, or early, depending on how you looked at it, Emil went over to where his phone was and typed out a message to Oskar, where he told him exactly what he told Luke he would, that Luke was as okay as he could be and that Emil would work to convince him to let his friends visit.

The path Luke was on would not be easy but Emil was now invested to make sure that Luke found his footing again, literally and figuratively.

Chapter Six

Luke

Luke had slept better last night than he had since he had woken from his coma. After the sound of the rain had lead to another nightmare, Luke had been surprised at how easy it had been to open up to Emil after the man had told him about his father's accident.

And there had been times last night when Luke was almost certain that Emil was flirting with him, but then Luke had chastised himself for being foolish to even consider such a daft idea. You only had to google Emil's name to see a barrage of images of Emil with stunning women.

Besides, Luke had like zero experience in that department. Sure, he'd kissed a few guys before, and then he started getting noticed by the media and Luke had pushed all that aside for the dream of being a world champion. He would never admit to anyone that he was lonely because then he would never have any peace.

His afternoon physio session had been halted because Luke had to attend a therapy session that was mandated by Rebel Racers. Luke had wheeled himself down to the therapist's office and had now sat for ten minutes in silence as the woman behind the desk studied him.

After more time ticked by, Doctor Chen sighed and asked Luke how he was feeling.

"Never better....now can I get back to the real work so I can get back in the car."

"The nurse on duty last night said you had trouble getting to sleep and spent time out on the balcony.."

Luke spun his chair around to look out the window as he massaged the muscle in his thigh that was aching after doing seven rounds this morning. "It was the rain." He admitted, knowing he had to give the woman something to report back to Charlie at Rebel Racers.

"What was the rain, Luke?"

"What kept me awake? I thought I was back in the car and crashing again. It's ironic that it took a freak storm in one of the world's hottest countries where it typically doesn't rain to almost kill me."

The psychologist wrote some notes in her little book. "I also hear that you are isolating yourself from friends and family. That doesn't strike me as healthy.

Being around friends and family can help you come to terms with the aftermath of your accident."

Luke wasn't sure that was the case for him. Everyone had their way of dealing with stress. Drivers all had their own rituals before a qualifying or a race. Quinn listened to music as loud as possible, only certain songs, to drown out the noise in the garage. Noah practised his reaction time and sparred. And Luke, he liked to listen to music too and dance around his side of the garage. He wasn't the best dancer but it helped him relax and destress.

"I worry that you are isolating yourself."

"I'm not." Luke blurted out, rubbing his thigh again. "I need some space to deal with everything and my family, my friends, I love them but they can be overwhelming at times. I just need time and look, I'm having dinner with another patient tonight so I'm not isolating myself."

The therapist gave Luke some homework and he tried very hard not to roll his eyes. It was early in the afternoon and he wasn't ready to go back to his room just yet. Luke wheeled himself into one of the common areas. He thought about what Emil had said last night. He pulled out his phone and texted Luna to say he was sorry for their fight and that it was okay if she wanted to come visit him soon.

Luke checked the time before he pressed his speed dial, the phone ringing and Luke second-guessed himself about making the call and was about to hang up when he heard a voice at the other end of the line.

"Hello?"

Hearing Noah's voice, having heard him call his name before he passed out in the car, made him shudder and he couldn't find his voice.

"Hello...is someone there?"

Luke realized that he must have his caller ID blocked because Noah didn't know that it was Luke on the other end. Noah sighed and Luke could almost see him rolling his eyes as he said he was about to hang up.

"Hey, it's me...Luke."

There was a stunned silence before he heard Noah speak. "Damn, brother, it's so fucking good to hear your voice."

Luke ran his hand down his face. "I'm ...I'm ...sorry I haven't called before but..."

"It's okay, Luke. It's okay. I understand."

They lapsed into silence, neither of them knowing exactly what to say but then Noah started talking about flying back between races to see him, and then Luke felt his head spinning.

"Can you give me a little more time? Please Noah? I need some more time. I don't want you guys to see me like this...to see me ...broken."

His voice cracked on the last word even as Noah started to talk.

"Luke, you're not broken. You're a little black and

blue but never broken. I can wait. I'll tell Quinn you called, but she would really love to hear your voice too."

"Noah, I..." Luke started and then cleared his voice. "Not right now. I just need to breathe and get my head right and then you can come and make a fuss. I really shouldn't have called."

"Luke," Noah's stern tone came down the line. "Day or night, you call me. I will always answer."

Luke hung up the phone without saying goodbye, not answering when it vibrated in his hand. He shoved it into his pocket and stared out the window until it grew dark and Luke numbly wheeled himself back to his room, stopping dead when he saw Emil waiting there, the scent of Chinese food making his stomach rumble.

Emil was taking food out of a bag and laying it out on the table. He was dressed in a short-sleeved tee in royal blue, and shorts that showed off the muscles on his calves and strong thighs. And he was barefoot.

The man turned to look at Luke and he smiled, illuminating his face as he grinned. "I couldn't find you so I called Quinn and asked her what kind of Chinese food you liked. I had a craving and I normally don't get to deviate from my diet. I hope you don't mind."

Emil beckoned him over, and Luke wheeled his chair over and lifted himself out of the chair and into the seat. His mouth watered at the sight of all the food and because of the man sitting across from him.

"I never had Chinese food until I moved to the UK to play soccer. The team put me up in this apartment next door to a Chinese gymnast and he and I used to have cheat days, where he would cook all these amazing meals. I would bring the Danish beer and ice cream. It was a fair trade if you ask me."

Luke laughed, shaking his head. "Pity we couldn't sneak some beers in. It's been, bloody hell, it's nearly been six months since I had a beer."

Emil grinned and reached down beside his chair. "Good thing I'm such a loveable rogue that I managed to persuade someone to grab two bottles. Only one each mind, as we are recovering from injury."

Emil handed him a beer, Luke ignoring the spark of electricity that surged through him the moment their fingers grazed each other's. They fell into an easy conversation as they ate, talking about sports and movies and everything in between. Emil asked him about places he would like to visit, once he was able, and asked Luke his opinion on places to go.

For the first time in a long time, Luke forgot that his legs didn't work right, that this was not his home, and his future was uncertain. He was just a guy eating dinner with a guy who was laughing at his stupid jokes and teasing him about his taste in movies. He tried not to think of the little niggling fact that Emil was only being friendly because Oskar had asked him to.

When the food was finished and their beers were gone, Luke was overwhelmed with a wave of sadness and a resounding knowledge that he did not want to be alone all night rehashing disastrous outcomes.

Emil must have sensed his change in demeanour because he reached for the remote control and pulled his chair over closer to where Luke sat, even though they could have gone and sat on the couch, asking Luke if he wanted to watch a movie with him.

And with the growing feeling in his chest, Luke knew that Emil could have asked anything of him and he would have done so if it meant he stayed just a little bit longer, even though Luke knew that any feelings he might be having were wasted on a man who could never reciprocate.

CHAPTER SEVEN

Luke

THE NEXT WEEK passed in a blur of physio sessions and evenings spent in Emil's company. It was strange how easily they had slipped into a routine. Luke told himself that it was down to the fact that as athletes, routine was in their bones and it was just simple to follow the pattern that had developed.

But the more time Luke spent with Emil the more he started to wonder if this was what it was like to have a relationship with someone. He wanted to understand what it was like to come home to someone and talk about your day. To have a partner in your life.

Luke knew he was being stupid, knew he was

falling for a man who could never be his but the more time he spent with Emil, the more he wanted him.

And Luke had made progress, not much, but enough where his physio said if he kept it up that in a week or two, he could lose the chair and start getting around with a walking frame or crutches. The pain in his hips had lessened and the leg cramps also, but there was still residual pain. He knew he would push through it, knew that he would fight anything to be fit again to get back in his car.

Everyone knew that Noah and Quinn had complicated upbringings and their journey to get where they were today and Luke, damn, Luke knew they deserved their happiness now and he didn't begrudge them that. But, everyone thought that Luke had it easy; two loving parents, a twin who was a force of nature, and friends that loved him.

They didn't understand that keeping a very big part of who he was in the shadows had been hard. Having to keep his secret had made it harder to trust, and more difficult to let anyone in. Luke didn't have the same experiences as his peers. He couldn't march in a pride parade, he couldn't go to gay bars and kiss a stranger.

Coming out to his parents, especially his Da had been the most nerve-wracking. Luna had known, had always known because the bond they shared meant there were no secrets between them. When Luke had told Luna, back when they were kids, she had laughed and said now they could go looking for boys together.

But his parents - Luke had been afraid of disappointing them. His Ma had always made it clear she wanted a brood of grandkids and Luke could be depriving her of that. As Luke wheeled himself back to his room after physio he couldn't help but think about when he came out to his parents when he was fourteen.

Luke was wiping down the kitchen table after dinner, his mother boiling the kettle to make tea. His heart was beating so hard in his chest and he had barely ate any of his dinner because he was so nervous. Luna had pushed him to be open with his parents and Luna was like a dog with a bone when she got the idea in her head.

It all came about when Luke had kissed a boy at a party and told Luna. It had affirmed what Luke had always known, that he was gay and he was terrified that his parents wouldn't understand.

"Luke, what's the matter, luv."

Luke lifted his eyes up to see his Ma looking at him with worried eyes and he wanted to tell her it was nothing and he was just tired but his anxiety forced the words to tumble from his lips.

"I like boys."

His mother froze for a minute and it was on the tip of his tongue to say he was only joking and take it back but then his mother was hugging him to her. "My sweet boy, you know I love you."

"But..." Luke began but his mother cut across him.

"No buts. There will never be anything that you tell me that will make me stop loving you. Do you hear me?"

Luke felt tears slip free and soon both himself and his mam were crying and the sound of it drew his dad into the kitchen.

"What's all this about?" Mick, his dad, asked in that deep voice of his and Luke tensed.

He stepped away from his mother and swiped at his eyes. "It's nothing."

Mick looked at his wife and then back at Luke. "Sure doesn't look like nothing to me."

His mother took his hand, and gave it a squeeze. "It's okay. Tell your dad what you told me."

His father was an imposing figure, broad and wide with the air of authority that was needed to run a bar and deal with drunk people every night. Luke had never been afraid of his father though, and he wasn't now. He was just afraid of his reaction.

Somehow, with his mother holding his hand, Luke summoned the courage to say. "I'm gay."

His father looked at him for a second and Luke thought his heart was going to jump out of his chest. His mouth was dry and he felt his body tremble as his dad took a breath.

"Is that all?" Mick asked, flicking on the kettle again to make fresh tea. "I'll tell ya the same thing I told

your sister. If you bring home a boy I don't like, then be prepared for me to tell ya so. I'm not afraid to say it when a boy isn't good enough for my son."

Luke hadn't been able to stop the sob from escaping from him, the relief of telling his parents enough to buckle his knees and it was his dad who caught him, strong arms around him as Luke cried and his dad brushed a hand over his hair.

His parents had accepted him and it had made life easier for a time. He knew there were a lot of other people in his situation that weren't as lucky as Luke was. They had supported him when he decided to keep his sexuality a secret from the public so they could focus on his driving. His parents were with him when he came out to Philip Coyle, the previous owner of Rebel Racers. He had told Noah, his fellow racer, and Noah had just shrugged and it was a nonissue.

Quinn had figured it out for herself when she had arrived and after a prickly first couple of weeks, she had warmed to him the moment she realized that Luke would never try and make a pass at her.

The thought made Luke smile as he resolved to message Quinn to check in after checking with Emil in case Quinn and Oskar had plans that he might inter-rupt. Luke was so caught up that he didn't notice the figure standing in his room until he had wheeled himself in.

Luna Sullivan stood looking out the window, her dyed red blood red hair masking the ginger that they had both inherited. A drummer in the band Heartache Melody, Luna was as extroverted as he was introverted. Today, Luna wore skin-tight leggings and crop top with a shirt thrown over it, and a pair of black boots.

She looked at Luke cautiously and folded her arms across her chest before Luke noticed the bandage around her hand and wrist.

"What happened to you?"

Luna dismissed him with a wave of her hand. "Oh, that's nothing. Had a fall. I'll be grand in a few weeks."

Luke knew his twin well enough to know when she was lying but he didn't push her. If you pushed Luna too much, she sure as hell pushed back and as someone who had pushed his friends and family away, he couldn't be one to judge. He trusted that Luna would tell him when she was ready and if it was worse than she was letting on.

"You look better."

Luke wheeled himself over to where Luna was standing. "I'm making progress. Might be able to lose the chair in a couple of weeks."

"That's great, Luke. Really great."

Even after their worst fights, it had never been as awkward as it was now.

"I need to talk- "

"I'm glad you- "

They spoke at the same time and then they laughed, easing some of the tension but then Luna sighed. "I need to talk to you Luke, and I need you to listen."

Luke already felt defensive and Luna hadn't even told him what was on her mind.

"Go on." Luke ground out, resting his hands in his lap as Luna shifted to look directly at him.

"I don't want to argue with you. I didn't come for another fight. But you have to stop being so selfish. There are a lot of people who want to help you and who are struggling to deal with what happened to you. You need to stop shutting them out and stop being a damn martyr."

Luke felt the anger inside him explode at Luna's words and he opened his mouth to give her a piece of his mind.

CHAPTER EIGHT

Emil

EMIL HEARD the shouting the moment he stepped off the elevator, finally free of his crutches, and he walked toward the sound of the raised voices. He heard Luke tell someone to get down off their high horse and then a female voice told Luke that anyone would think he liked playing the martyr.

The nurses around the desk all looked in a state of shock as if they didn't know what to do but Emil smiled and told them he would sort it. He strode over to Luke's bedroom, pausing in the doorway as he took in the scene.

A woman with outrageous red hair was glaring down at Luke with her hands on her hips, her features so similar to the man that Emil had grown more fond of that he wanted to admit, that Emil knew the woman had to be Luke's twin sister Luna. They were so embroiled in their argument that they didn't even notice Emil standing in the doorway.

"You are loving the way people are running around fretting over you and I'm sick of you hurting our parents. Hurting Quinn. You can't blame us all for the fact you crashed, Luke. You crashed the car."

"Oh fuck off, Luna!" Luke snarled, his fists clenched and unclenched in his lap. "I didn't put myself in the wall. I didn't put myself in a coma for attention. You must not have watched the goddamn crash because I certainly wouldn't have done all this to myself."

"Oh, I watched the crash. Luke. I've seen it over and over. I've heard Noah and Quinn tell me just how lucky you are to be alive and you keep on pushing to do it all over again. Mam is beside herself that the next time, she'll be burying you!"

Luke beat a hand against his chest. "I can't help with that. I *have* to get better. I *have* to get back in the car. It's all I have, Luna. It's all I fucking have and if I lose it, then I lose everything. I thought you would understand. I thought you would have my back. If you had to give up drumming, what else would you do? What else can I do if I'm not driving a goddamn car!"

"Oh give me a break. For years it's been all about you and the F1 dream. When you had karting competitions, I had to miss out. I had to trek around the world to follow your dream."

Luke lunged forward, almost forgetting about his chair and Emil to a step further into the room. "Oh, poor little princess having to fly all around the world because your brother had races. What about all the times I went alone when you had a shitty back alley pub gig and the parents wanted to go to support you? I wasn't the only one, Luna, who was supported by our parents so don't act the fucking victim."

You could cut the atmosphere with a knife even if Emil considered that the siblings' words were cutting as deep as any blade. Emil moved further into the room and it was then Luna spotted him and she glared at Emil.

"Who the hell are you?"

"Don't talk to him like that!" Luke exclaimed, glancing over at Emil, a blush on his cheeks.

Emil turned on the charm, flashing a bright smile. "Emil Anderson. You must be Luna."

The woman narrowed as she inspected him. "Emil? Oskar's friend Emil."

Emil bent at the waist, giving a little bow before he grinned. "Depends on what Oskar has told you about me."

Luna folded her arms across her chest. "Quinn told me you were charming and funny and handsome."

"Quinn is a very intelligent woman." Emil teased and that made Luna laugh.

Emil snuck a glance at Luke, who was white-knuckling the arms of his wheelchair and his face was unreadable, even if there was a flash of emotion in his emerald-green eyes. What was it...jealously? Was Luke thinking that he was flirting with his sister?

"Luna was just leaving." Luke ground out, turning in his chair and wheeling himself to the door to the balcony, and then he was gone, leaving Emil alone with Luna.

"Ugh, he can be so fucking stubborn," Luna remarked with a sigh.

"I have a feeling that is a family trait," Emil said with a smile.

Luna studied him, then glanced from Emil to where Luke was out on the balcony. Her eyes widened then she smiled as if she had figured something out, then she strode over to where Emil was standing and lightly touched his arm.

"My brother might be stubborn but sometimes he can be oblivious to what's going on around him. He can be too focused on driving to see but I do."

Emil felt his throat dry up. "I have no idea what you mean."

The woman smiled, winking. "Course you don't. But I tell ya something, Mr. Emil Anderson, if you hurt my brother, you'll end up back on crutches."

"Again, I have no idea what you are inferring"

Luna looked back to where her twin was then back at Emil. "Whatever you say. He's got the biggest heart, my brother."

"You were fighting a moment ago."

Luna shrugged, snorting. "We are twins. We fight a lot. But that doesn't mean I don't want him to be happy even when he's being an ass."

She walked over and knocked on the window to wave at Luke and Luke waved back, a frown on his face. Luna rolled her eyes as she headed for the door, pausing when Emil called her name.

Emil ran a hand through his hair. "Oskar doesn't know. About me."

Luna's eyes widened, a small smile curving her hips. "Does Luke?"

Emil shook his head, not sure why he was telling Luna something he could not tell his closest friend. It wasn't that he was ashamed of who he was, but it would absolutely shatter him if Oskar looked at him differently.

"I won't say a thing. But I've spent some time with Oskar and he knows all about Luke. I think he would be glad that you felt comfortable telling him."

Luna left then, sparing once more glance for her brother before she disappeared down the hall. Emil took a moment to gather himself before he followed Luke out into the fresh air.

"Your sister is like a tornado."

Luke didn't say anything in response, just continued to look out over the city as Emil flopped down on a chair beside him. "So, you are ignoring me now?"

"I don't really have anything to say. I certainly

don't want to listen to you talk about you flirting with my sister."

"If you think that was flirting, then you have obviously not been flirted with enough."

Luke flinched like Emil had punched him and blushed a shade of red to his cheeks that told Emil that his words had embarrassed him. Emil sighed, scooting to the edge of his chair

"I have no designs on your sister. I was defusing an argument. Why are you angry with me now?"

"I'm not."

"Yes, you are. Just spit it out so we can forget all the unpleasantness and have a nice civil dinner."

Luke snapped his head toward Emil and Emil saw what could only be described as fire in the other man's eyes. "Don't patronize me and treat me like a child."

"Then do not behave like one."

Emil knew there and then that he had pushed too hard and he saw the moment Luke just shut down. He made to try and smooth things over with Luke but the other man looked defeated.

"Luke, I am sorry. Let us forget the unpleasantness and enjoy a nice meal together."

"I've lost my appetite," Luke replied, turning his chair in the direction of his room and moving away from Emil.

"Luke, stop," Emil explained as he got to his feet, as Luke stopped with his escape plans. "Why does it bother you so much if I flirted with Luna? I was trying to get her to stop yelling at you."

"You know why." Luke proclaimed darkly to which Emil shook his head.

"I do not. Explain it to me."

Luke was silent for a few heartbeats, then his shoulders slumped and Emil knew that there would be no truths shared this night.

"It doesn't matter. I'm tired. I'm gonna go to bed."

It was on the tip of Emil's tongue to ask Luke if he wanted company but he did not think that his attempts at humour would do much to drag Luke from his bad mood. Instead, Emil watched as Luke wheeled himself back into his room, closed the door, and shut the blinds, blocking Emil's view and Emil had not expected such a mundane act to hit him as much as it did. It felt like a dismissal, one that did not sit well with Emil and gave him a night of restless sleeping.

CHAPTER NINE

Emil

LUKE HAD AVOIDED Emil for a couple of days now, and Emil was starting to get frustrated. He had tried to smooth over any residual unpleasantness, however, Luke had been too tired most nights to each dinner with him or watch a movie like they had done so many times before. Any interactions were brief and cordial but it was obvious that there was this new layer of distance between them.

Emil couldn't just stride into the room and tell Luke that he was attracted to him because Luke wasn't aware that Emil had figured out that Luke was gay. He didn't want to out him, even if his twin knew that her brother was gay as apparently did Oskar.

When Luna had said that to Emil, it had struck a chord with Emil and he knew that he would have to be upfront with Oskar in order to be his authentic self. If this attraction to Luke was going to go anywhere, Emil wanted to be honest with his closest friend.

But Oskar had enough to deal with this weekend. During a rare week off in the race calendar, Oskar had taken Quinn home to Denmark to meet his mother. Oskar was nervous because he wanted Alma to love Quinn as much as Oskar did, but knowing Alma, she would welcome Quinn with an open heart and open arms if she was feeling like herself today.

Before her dementia had captured her mind, Alma always had time for a hug, for a wise word, and a shoulder when needed. Alma had been one of the first people he had shared the most private part of himself and she said she had known, that it did not matter if Emil liked men or women or both what mattered was the love in his heart and that he went out in the world and shared it as much as possible.

Her husband, Viggo, Oskar's father had always been a bitter man who was more fond of Alma's money than his wife. No one could understand why Alma had fallen for Viggo but everyone who loved Alma had been disgusted when Viggo abandoned his wife and son when her illness became too difficult for him to bear.

Viggo was now expecting a child with a woman the same age as his son any day now, and Emil always thought Viggo was a vain man chasing the youth he no longer had.

Oskar's father had despised Emil and Emil's family for not being privileged enough to associate with his well-to-do family. Emil had overheard him complaining that the house reeked of fish anytime Emil visited and it was Alma that chastised her husband.

After Emil was scouted and gained some notoriety playing for his country, Viggo had been more than happy to invite Emil to dinners, especially when Emil played for one of the London clubs during his teens. Emil had signed for the team for many reasons, but one was to be near Oskar who was studying at a boarding school nearby. Despite many an invite to attend dinners with Viggo's friends, Emil had always politely declined and it annoyed Viggo to no end when he and Oskar were snapped by the media eating at dive bars or less than fancy restaurants in an obvious snub to the man who was a desperate man clinging to the prestige and wealth his wife's money had afforded him.

Emil knew that over the years, Oskar as his mother's medical proxy and executor of her estate had cut off Viggo's handouts and it had forced Viggo to have it out with Oskar in front of Quinn.

Quinn was very much in agreement with Emil that Viggo was an asshole.

Emil glanced over toward the closed door across the hall, wondering if he should just bite the bullet and just confront Luke about the new distance between them but Emil had stopped. Mark, Luke's physio, had told Emil that Luke had a difficult day today and when he had checked on him a while ago, the race car driver was out cold.

So Emil had left Luke to his rest and called his team doctor to update him on his progress and plans were made for his return to Denmark and finally get back to what he was best at. The news should have elated him but there was something that made him reluctant to set a date to return.

However, Emil had spent some time over the last few days considering what acting on his attraction to Luke would mean. Luke was very much still hiding who he was and while Emil certainly wasn't fully out of the closet, he was not going to hide a relationship. Would Luke ever feel comfortable enough to hold his hand in public or would they simply ignore each other as if there was nothing between them?

Thinking that far ahead seemed ludicrous especially when nothing had physically happened between himself and Luke, but emotionally, Emil was invested in Luke's recovery. It made him uncomfortable to think of not seeing him every day and over the last few days when they had not talked, or when they had, it was stilted and awkward, Emil had come away unhappy.

Emil was still pondering his dilemma late into the night and was so distracted that he almost missed his phone vibrating. Emil glanced at it, saw Oskar's name and picture come up. It was late for Oskar to call and

Emil had a sinking feeling as he grabbed it and answered.

"Oskar, what is it?"

There was silence on the other end of the phone and Emil knew before Oskar spoke what his friend was having so much difficulty in saying. But he knew, like when Emil has lost his father a few years ago, that Oskar needed to process this himself and that involved saying it out loud, even as tears filled his own eyes.

"She was in such good spirits, Emil. It was like having her back to the person she was before the dementia. She laughed and smiled and told Quinn all the old stories of you and me. She was more herself than she had been in a long time"

Emil's heart broke for his friend, wishing he was there to embrace him but Emil knew Quinn was there to look after him. He was glad that Oskar was not alone.

"She is gone, Emil. Min mor has fallen asleep and will never wake up. She went to sleep holding me in her arms and as she took her final breath, she smiled as if she was in no more pain."

Oskar sobbed down the phone, not a man totally at peace with his emotions and Emil was crying with him, in their shared grief for a woman who was as gentle as the first snowfall of winter and who shone brighter than any star that ever shone.

"She is at peace, Oskar. She waited long enough to know that you were not alone and she went on her own terms. She will be missed and she will always be loved."

Oskar did not answer him and soon, Quinn took the phone and spoke gently to Emil. "Hey, it's Quinn. You were the first person he called, the first person he wanted to call. He said Alma would want her two sons to comfort one another but hearing your voice has set him off. Are you okay, Emil?"

To hear that Oskar and Alma in turn considered him family was heart-breaking and he hoped that Alma knew just how much she meant to him.

"I can book a flight over ...if he needs me."

It was more like Emil needed to see Oskar rather than the other way around but Oskar would need him in the days and weeks to come, not just in that moment.

Quinn was quiet for a second and Emil heard her close a door. "Alma wanted to be cremated and some of her ashes scattered in Denmark and some in Ireland so Oskar would have a place to go. We will do the Denmark part in the next day or two or something and then come back to Ireland to scatter the ashes. Oskar wants you there for that."

"You'll look after him for me?" Emil had to clear his throat after he asked, knowing that Quinn would be a steady presence for his chosen brother.

"Of course I will. Is there anyone who can look after you, Emil?"

That was the million euro question and Emil

laughed it off, telling Quinn he would be okay before they ended the call and Emil sat in the darkness, not knowing what to do with himself now.

He would have given anything to be with Oskar in this moment and not alone in a foreign country by himself. Emil walked over to the window and sat down on the sofa, gazing into the night as he allowed the tears to flow freely now.

"Sleep well, dearest Alma. Until we meet again."

CHAPTER TEN

Luke

LUKE HAD THROWN himself into building the strength in his legs and the physio had finally allowed him to try out some of the machines. He had done leg curls and a few reps on the rowing machine, building up his resistance and he was surprised by how much he was able to do.

He was also surprised by how tired he felt after the new intense workout. There had been times when he had done a full day of working out, then a few laps in the car, and then gone on a night out, or pulled a full shift at the family bar, and still not been as tired as he was now.

Mark had explained that he needed to up his

calorie intake as he was burning off some serious energy with the new routine. Sleep was also important apparently and considering Luke was actively avoiding Emil, trying to get more sleep was as good an excuse as any.

When Luke woke in the dead of night, he decided now was the perfect time to try and do a little stroll with the walking frame to get him used to being upright. He'd been practicing all week with the frame and could now do short distances. The prognosis was for him getting rid of the frame altogether in a few weeks.

Luke got out of bed and reached from the frame, taking a breath before he put one foot in front of the other and shuffled toward the hallway. He found it easier to move with the frame when there were no eyes on him and at this hour, the halls empty and still.

Or so he thought.

The sound of crying from Emil's room made him change course and he pushed open the door of Emil's bedroom. Emil was sitting on the couch with his head in his hands, crying so hard that he didn't even hear Luke come into the room. It was only when Luke awkwardly shuffled with the frame that Emil jerked his head up and Luke stopped breathing.

Emil's eyes were puffy and red as if he had been crying for some time and he looked so lost. He opened his mouth to speak but only a sob escaped his lips before the tears flowed again. Luke worked his way over to the couch as quickly as he could and sat down beside Emil, wrapping his arms around the other man. Emil clung to him, burying his face in Luke's shoulder.

Luke simply held Emil as he cried, his heartbeat racing as he muttered that everything was okay, and to let it all out. Luke stroked his hair, the intimacy not lost on Luke but Emil clung to him for what seemed like hours.

Emil lifted his head and Luke dropped his hands as Emil rubbed his face and looked at him, "I'm sorry."

Luke reached out and gave his leg a squeeze. "Hey, don't apologize. I'm here to listen as your friend."

"Are we friends then?" Emil said with a short laugh.

"Of course we are," Luke assured him, but even to himself, it tasted like lies because Luke wanted more with Emil than was possible.

Emil leaned back on the couch and Luke positioned himself so he was looking at Emil. Their knees were touching and Emil's dark eyes were looking at him and when he spoke, Luke could hear the emotion in his tone.

"When I was eleven, we had little or no money. My father was disabled and the money I made at the weekends on the fishing boat helped feed my sisters and clothe them for school. I went without so they didn't have to. During the winter, my boots broke and I glued them back together but the wetness seeped in."

Luke felt a wave of sadness course through him

and he reached out and took Emil's hand in his. It felt natural; it felt right.

"I was in pain but I tried to pretend I was okay. I was scared. I knew If I got frostbite, then I would lose the career I wanted more than life itself and I was on the cusp of losing everything because I had to spend my days on a fishing boat like my father. I went to Oskar's house and his mother, the wonderful Alma, forced me to look after my feet and gave me a pair of boots. I didn't know how to thank her because I could not pay her back but do you know what she said to me? She said – "my darling son, your feet one day will take you all over the world. One day, you will come and tell me all the adventures you've had, and then the debt will be repaid."

A tear slipped down Emil's cheek and without thinking, Luke reached out with his other hand and wiped the tear away. Emil's breath hitched and Luke, Luke wasn't sure what the hell was going on in this moment.

"She hadn't slipped too far into the disease when I made the Danish team. I scored a goal on my debut and when I pulled off my jersey to celebrate, I had this one's for you Alma on my vest. She had it framed next to Oskar's military photo. I only wanted to make her proud."

"What's happened, Emil? Tell me what happened."

It took Emil a few minutes and a few deep breaths

before he could speak but Luke would just wait for Emil to be ready, even if it took all night.

"Oskar took Quinn to meet his mother. He was there with her when she passed. I didn't get to say goodbye. She was responsible for pushing me and feeding me. She loved me unconditionally and I just wish I could have said goodbye, even if she didn't know me, I would have wanted to tell her I loved her one more time."

"Emil," Luke said as he gripped his hand tighter. "She knew you loved her and from the sounds of it, she loved you too. The picture on the wall was only a small part. And I am sorry that you didn't get to see her one last time, and I truly am sorry for your loss."

Emil entwined his fingers tighter with Luke's, his eyes on him and Luke's heart felt like it was going to explode from his chest. He didn't know when it happened when his attraction had turned to something deeper, but the way Emil was looking at him now, it tightened Luke's body, and considering that Emil was grieving, it was a completely inappropriate train of thought that Luke was heading down toward and he chastised himself.

"I know that we are not on the best of terms at the moment," Emil said, still holding on to Luke's hand, "But I am grateful that you are here. I did not want to be alone."

"I will always be here for you, even when we are released from this prison."

Emil chuckled and he smiled, reaching out to caress Luke's face. "You are a good man, Luke Sullivan. A very good man."

Luke's heartbeat was pounding in his ears, the weight of Emil's hand on his face was so searing it almost scalded him and before Luke could form a logical thought, he leaned in and pressed his lips to Emil's. His lips were soft and warm and Luke felt his body come alive and he craved more.

Luke reached out to take Emil's face in his hands when Emil jerked back and Luke realized he had made a terrible mistake. Emil looked startled, utterly shocked at what Luke had just done, and Luke couldn't blame him. He was an idiot, an absolute idiot.

"Oh god, oh shit...I'm so sorry. I didn't mean it...fuck... I'm sorry."

Luke lunged upright, grabbing hold of his frame and ignoring the flare of pain in his hip and he tried to make a quick exit, heat flushing his face with embarrassment. He stumbled as he made it to the door, ignoring Emil as he tried to get him to stop.

"It's okay, Luke. Come back and we can talk about it."

"I made a mistake. I'm sorry. I made a mistake."

If Luke could have run away from his shame and embarrassment, he would have run right out of there. His lips tingled from the aftermath of the kiss and his body was thrumming as he slammed the door to his room closed and leaned his head against it.

What had possessed him to just kiss Emil like that? Luke knew what it was like to have feelings for someone and not act on them but when he was around Emil, it made him want to throw caution to the wind and indulge in every fantasy that bounced around in his head.

But after seeing the revolution in Emil's eyes at the kiss, Luke knew that Emil could never return his feelings. Luke had never had such a devasting lapse in control that could threaten to unravel everything that he had built. If Emil told anyone about the kiss, Luke's secret could be exposed and the media circus would be never-ending.

Luke cradled his head in his hands.

How the hell could he have been so stupid?

CHAPTER ELEVEN

Luke

LUKE HAD BEEN AVOIDING Emil the past couple of days, so he had been relieved to find out that Emil had left the rehab facility for the day to scatter Oskar's mother's ashes. He spent the time in the gym, using his need to get back solely on two feet to distract himself from the utter embarrassment of what he had done.

It didn't help that every time Luke's mind strayed to just how good the kiss had felt before he realized the colossal mistake he had made. His body reacted, and Luke had to go to the shower, turn it on as cold as he could, and when that didn't help, he had to take matters into his own hand...pardon the pun.

For the first time since he woke up from his coma that he missed having someone to talk to. Luna was always his go-to when he needed to vent, and so were

Noah and Quinn. They always knew how to cheer him up or just be there for him but in this, he had no one to call or ask advice to.

He actually wouldn't have minded a hug from his Ma either.

Today Luke had spent the morning sweating it out in the gym and then he went for a swim in the pool. The water gave him the freedom to move and because his arms were still stronger than his legs at the moment, threading the water made him feel like he was normal again. It was stupid really, but with all the shit in his head, Luke would take any semblance of normality that he could grab hold of.

Luke went and took another shower, pulling on a loose tracksuit bottom and a tee when Mark arrived and asked Luke to come for a new updated MRI to see just check on everything. It was hopefully another step in him getting back to normal and out of this place.

The MRI in itself was relatively painless and then Luke had taken another walk around the corridors while he waited for the team of doctors to mull over his MRI and give him an update. He had done a full lap of the reception area when he noticed a woman walking into the rehab centre that Luke hadn't been expecting to see.

Charlotte "Charlie" Coyle was his boss, owner, and CEO of Rebel Racers. She had her long black hair pulled back into a ponytail, showing off her pale skin and warm smile as she came towards him. She wore dark jeans and a tee, a teal-coloured blazer thrown on over, and the moment she came closer to Luke, he saw the diamond ring around her neck.

"I cannot tell you how good it is to see you upright." Charlie grinned as she held out her hands to embrace him and Luke braced one hand on the walker, then hugged Charlie tightly.

"I'm just pacing the floor while the doctors have a look at my most recent MRI. Not exactly a jog around the racetrack but it won't be long before Noah is forcing his obsession on me again."

Charlie laughed, falling into step with him as Luke continued with his shuffle. Luke listened as Charlie told him all the news, careful to avoid any mention of his race seat. Luke knew it was coming, that the year was passing by so quickly and he realistically had until Christmas to be in with a fighting chance at regaining his seat. That was only three months really to prove everyone wrong.

"Where's Noah today? I didn't realize ye were back in Ireland."

"Noah's still away," Charlie replied with a warm smile. "He has some charity event before the next race. He'll be home after the doubleheader. If it's okay, then maybe he could come and see you properly. He told me ye spoke on the phone."

"Okay, sure. I'd like to see him."

That made Charlie smile even wider. "He frets. He likes to pretend he's all chiselled jaw and broody good looks and tough as nails but I know he worries. He's so protective over you and Quinn, like the big brother he never got to be. I don't think we would have gotten through the first few weeks after the crash without him. It almost killed him leaving you in the hospital. He wanted to be there when you woke up."

Luke felt heat on his cheeks. "It was better he wasn't there. I wasn't at my best when I did wake up. I'd like to blame it on the pain meds and stuff but I just ... yano."

Charlie reached over and rested her hand on his. "I understand. And Noah does too. I told him that he would be exactly the same if it was him. You race car drivers are stubborn."

When they reached the end of the hall, Charlie stopped and asked Luke to sit down. Luke lowered himself down on the seat and looked at Charlie, her green eyes suddenly very sombre.

"Luke, I'm gonna have to put aside your friend, Charlie, for the next couple of minutes and just be your boss. I've been putting this off for a couple of days and time is running out."

Luke's palms were suddenly very sweaty, his stomach rolled and his heart, it was beating as hard as Luna's drums. He couldn't hear this...he couldn't hear this, not now...

"Please, Charlie..."

Charlie cleared her throat. "At the moment, some of the other teams are trying to pull Quinn away with lucrative deals and promises of a fast car. She's a future world champion and she deserves to win that for Rebel Racers. I'm going to offer her a new one-year deal to partner Noah next year."

"No, please, Charlie. Don't give up on me. Please don't take my seat away from me."

Charlie shook her head, and Luke saw tears in her eyes. "I'm not. I promise you. I'm giving you a little more time to get back to fighting fit. Once you've recuperated, we can revisit the seat allocation. This was not an easy decision, but my father would turn in his grave if he thought I let Quinn leave Rebel Racers. You are still very much a part of the team, Luke."

Luke felt like his world was crumbling down around him. The only thing that had kept his head above water had been the knowledge that he would get back in that car, and now Charlie was setting fire to the tiny shreds of hope that he'd clung to.

He surged to his feet and grabbed his walker, and Charlie followed him. Mark opened the door to the consultants' room and called them in. Luke ambled forward, his eyes darting to Charlie as she looked at him with an expression that could only be described as pity.

"They asked me to come in too."

Luke numbly entered the room, listening as they all told him that he had made remarkable progress and he should be proud of how far he had come in such a short space of time. There was lots of medical jargon and then the doctor asked Luke if he had heard what he said and Luke had to admit that he hadn't and asked him to repeat it.

"After an extensive amount of tests, we can confirm that there is some small inflammation in your right hip. We think it's an infection. We want to give you some antibiotics and keep an eye on it, but it does slow the timeline down a little. It's not a setback, Luke, it's just a bump in the road."

Luke got to his feet then, nodding when he was asked by Mark if he understood what the inflammation meant. He left without saying a word, not stopping when Charlie called his name because he just couldn't deal with any more bad news.

His mother had always said that bad things happen in threes.

He really wasn't expecting to be ambushed by a fourth the moment he returned to his room, especially since he was a couple of seconds away from losing his shit and having a complete breakdown. He had been so distracted, moving on autopilot that he didn't realize that someone was already in his room when he walked in and closed the door, leaning his head against it.

Was it really bad of him that he wondered if he was still in the coma and this was some weird dream thing his subconscious had concurred up in a feeble attempt to... hell, he didn't know what.

A throat cleaned and his eyes darted open, then shifted to the petite woman standing by the open baloney door, her blue-black hair falling loose on her shoulders. Her face was guarded and it reminded him of the first time they had met when Philip introduced them and the short, fierce young girl had looked at him and Noah with such terrifying grit and residence that Luke had wanted to hug her.

Luke would never lay a finger on her: he would never have hurt her.

Except in that moment, right now, he felt his anger simmer, ready to explode.

Chapter Twelve

Emil

After the initial shock of Luke's kiss, Emil had been fully on board to explore it deeper but then the look Luke had gotten in his eyes of pure terror had doused any flames. The other man had fled from Emil, then avoided him for days. It had taken Emil some time to figure out that perhaps Luke was afraid that Emil might "out" him and with everything else, Luke probably didn't want to have to deal with that as well as his injuries.

Emil had waited outside the entrance to the facility, waiting for Oskar to arrive, letting his oldest and closet friend park and get out of the car. Emil went to him instantly, embracing Oskar and holding him close. Oskar looked tired, but that was to be expected.

Stepping out of the hug, Emil grasped his friend's

face in his eyes, his pale blue eyes filled with a grief that mirrored his own. "Valhalla has gained a true warrior. Though I selfishly wish we could have kept her longer."

Oskar offered Emil a sad smile. "She used to love when you would bound into the house and declare yourself to be a descendant of Vikings, and recite passages from the Poetic Edda. I think she would like to know that you have kept up the tradition."

They got into the car then, driving to one of the many places in Ireland Alma had planned on visiting and never had the chance. Emil wasn't sure how to bring up Oskar's father's reaction to his wife's death, but considering Viggo had tried to divorce Alma only a few months ago, Emil was certain the only thing Viggo was thinking about was any money he felt he was due.

"I had always known mother was prepared but she had it all planned; her cremation, her will, and all the legal stuff sorted. I had not much to do apart from following her instructions. It was nice, to think of her planning it all out knowing that I would be useless at all of it."

"I think our dear Alma simply did not want her baby to be stressed when she knew that it would be difficult enough just to say goodbye."

"Perhaps," Oskar said, though Emil could make out a hint of a smile that made the weight in his own chest feel lighter. Then Oskar's grip on the steering wheel tightened. "Viggo had the audacity to try and play the mourning husband."

Emil glanced at Oskar, then said. "I'm sure he gave a magnificent performance."

"Indeed," Oskar snorted, his shoulders relaxing slightly. "He seemed appalled that I had her cremated without waiting for him to offer an opinion, then even more so when the solicitor on the zoom call explained that the entirety of mother's estate had been left to me and me alone, his face turned a scarlet shade of red. Quinn said he looked like his head was about to explode."

Emile laughed at the thought of Viggo finally getting what he deserved in life. "I would have given my golden boot award to have seen his face."

"I'm pretty sure Quinn took a picture. I'm sure she would only be delighted to share it with you." Oskar retorted in that dry tone of his.

They both shared a much-needed laugh and then Emil waited as Oskar parked the car and they got out, Oskar taking the small urn that held Alma's ashes. Emil remembered the stunning aerial shot of the tiny church in Gougane Barra. Alma had said that she would have chosen to get married there if she could have because it looked like the most tranquil place in the world.

Nestled in a scenic valley in the Shehy Mountains of County Cork, Gougane Barra is at the source of the River Lee, including a lake with an oratory built on a small island and a forest surrounding it. Emil himself was never one for the quiet, but standing here in this marvel of scenery, Emil found himself feeling quite privileged.

Oskar began to walk toward where the church was, getting to the edge of the lake before he glanced around and looked at Emil. "I probably should have made certain that we can scatter her ashes here. She would be quite appalled if either of us ended up getting arrested."

"I would think Alma would roar with laughter at forcing us two to perform an illegal activity in her name, especially her by-the-book son. Me, I feel she would expect it of."

The bark of laughter that came out of Oskar had some of the other tourists glancing in their direction and Emil told Oskar to stop drawing attention to them or perhaps they might get arrested.

They sobered then and Emil stood shoulder to shoulder with Oskar as he opened the urn, offered up a few words in Danish before he let the wind sweep away Alma's ashes and then Oskar sank down on the grass and watched as her ashes floated to the water and that was it.

Emil followed him down, resting his hands behind him as he asked Oskar if he was okay.

"I wasn't but I will be. Thank you for coming with me."

"Oskar," Emil said, nudging his friend's shoulder. "There is no place I would rather be."

They sat in silence for a time, no words needed between them as they mourned a woman who had been so crucial in their lives, even after her memory began to fail. It was a relief that Alma was finally at peace now, and that Oskar could continue with the happiness he had found since he came to Ireland and found his Quinn. It was what Alma would have wanted.

As if Oskar knew the direction Emil's mind had gone, Oskar picked up a stone and tossed it into the river, skimming it across the water.

"My mother and Quinn hit it off right away. Quinn was nervous because she was afraid that she wasn't good enough but my mother hugged Quinn and asked her all about her tattoos. They locked themselves in her room for a good while and when Quinn came out, she'd been crying but wouldn't tell me what my mother had said."

"The ways of women have long since been lost to me. Best to leave them to their secrets."

When Oskar didn't laugh, Emil sighed, picking up a stone to skim it across the water himself.

"I should have known that she was too lucid, but I was just so thrilled that she and Quinn got on so well. I should have seen it. The doctors said that this can happen, that sometimes, a patient can have a burst of energy before they pass. I should have known."

"Alma would not have wanted you to know. It was exactly the way she wanted it to end, my friend. She would not have wanted to prologue your pain."

Oskar lifted his face, looking at the sky. "She called me to her art room the afternoon before she died. She asked me if Quinn made me as happy as it seemed and I told her that she did. She said she was glad and then she gave me a box and she made me promise that one day, in the future, when the time was right, that I give what was in the box to Quinn. When I opened the box, it was her mother's diamond engagement ring, the one she had worn herself."

Emil felt his heart break for Oskar in that moment, knowing Alma would have given anything to watch her son marry his soulmate, and by giving Oskar the ring, it had been a sure sign of Alma's approval.

"Do I need to sort out my best man suit?"

Oskar chuckled and rolled his eyes. "Not yet. One day. But not yet. There is no rush."

Emil grinned at Oskar, skimming another stone across the water as Oskar looked at him and his friend frowned.

"Mother did say something strange though."

"Strange?" Emil asked, wondering what Alma could have said to make Oskar think it was strange.

Oskar hmmmd in response. "Indeed. After she gave me the rings, she made me promise to make sure that you were okay. When I laughed and told her that was one person she never had to worry about, she was quite stern about me promising to look after you. That her other son needed to know that he too could be loved and accepted."

Emil's heart dropped to his stomach. He knew what Alma was trying to tell him from her words and her promise from Oskar. That she saw him and accepted him and loved him, as if Emil was her son too. His heart almost broke.

Oskar must have read something in his face because he reached out and grasped his shoulder. "You look as if you have the weight of the world on your shoulders, Emil. I knew it when I saw you this morning and I can see it now. it's more than grief; like you carry a great burden. Tell me what is on your mind?"

CHAPTER THIRTEEN

Luke

"WHAT ARE YOU DOING HERE?"

Luke hated how fragile his voice sounded, how frail he must look to Quinn as he was only able to stand there with the aid of the goddamn walker. And there she was standing in front of him, healthy and happy and exactly where he wanted to be. He knew he was a bastard for being jealous of the fact that while his world had been burning to ash, Quinn had been able to withstand the flames and she had taken his place.

Life had continued without him. People had moved on with their lives while he had been in stasis. Quinn had the career she always wanted, a handsome boyfriend, and a new home. Noah had a fiancée and was on the fast track to being a world champion.

He should be happy for them both because his two closest friends deserved to be happy and he wanted them to be, and yet, he was angry with them and with himself.

Formula 1 was a business, one that changed with every race. It was a constantly changing environment and drivers needed to keep up with the technology and the evolving nature of the cars. A driver who raced ten years ago might not be able to compete with the cars nowadays and the fitness required to be the best and line out as one of only twenty drivers. There was always someone younger, someone faster, someone *better* ready to replace you.

A year might not seem like a long time, but in the world of formula 1, it was an eternity.

"I came to see you," Quinn said, moving away from the open door and closing it, shutting out the cold. "It's so good to see you on your feet, Luke, it's amazing."

Quinn stepped forward like she wanted to hug him and Luke stop himself from flinching. That stopped Quinn from advancing, and it clenched Luke's heart because he knew just how hard it was for Quinn to show affection.

"She's a future world champion and she deserves to win that for Rebel Racers. I'm going to offer her a new one-year deal to partner Noah next year."

Charlie's words hit him again as Quinn leaned against the bed frame. "I wanted to check in before I flew out tomorrow. Oskar and Emil are having some time together so Oskar can scatter his mam's ashes. Have you seen much of Emil since he's been here?"

Luke couldn't stop the heat from flooding to his face and Quinn looked surprised. "Really? Well, I wasn't expecting that?"

It felt like Quinn was just here to mock him, to taunt him, and now, after the embarrassment of kissing Emil, it felt like insult to injury.

"I don't know why I bother telling them I don't want any fucking visitors when they keep letting everyone in. I'm tired, Quinn. I'm sure you have more important things to do than lurk around here."

"I just wanted to see how you were. I needed to see you, Luke."

Luke pushed away from the door and stepped to the side, his walker slipping across the floor. "Well, you've seen me now. Duty done. Hope that makes you feel better at least."

Quinn put her hands on her hips, anger, and sadness pricking her eyes. "What the fuck is wrong with you? Why are you mad at me?"

"Slow the timeline down a little. It's not a setback, Luke, it's just a bump in the road."

Blood rushed to his head and he felt dizzy. He tried to reign in the storm brewing inside him but it was getting extremely hard to hold his tongue.

"As I said, Quinn, I'm tired. So you can go and tell Charlie that you won, that I concede defeat. But don't come here and rub my face in it. Just go, Quinn, please go."

His voice broke and Quinn's eyes widened. "I don't understand, Luke. What's Charlie got to do with anything and what the hell are you talking about? Me winning? What have I won?"

"She's a future world champion and she deserves to win that for Rebel Racers. I'm going to offer her a new one-year deal to partner Noah next year."

"Just go, Quinn!" Luke screamed, clutching at his hair for fear he would lash out and he wanted to hurt himself, to feel anything but this unravelling, this feeling of being pulled apart and unable to steady himself.

"Don't you fucking shout at me, Luke Sullivan. I've spent the last few months worrying that you were going to die! Every single day that you didn't wake up was another day without you."

"Oh please," Luke snapped, shaking his head. "I played right into your hands, didn't I?"

"I don't know what's wrong with you or what you are trying to say, Luke."

Luke closed his eyes, tried to calm his mind. He wished Quinn would just leave and he could faintly hear her still talking to him but it felt like he was underwater, his ears filled with static until he heard

Quinn say. "Maybe I should go. I have an early flight in the morning."

"She's a future world champion and she deserves to win that for Rebel Racers. I'm going to offer her a new one-year deal to partner Noah next year."

The last thread of his restraint snapped and his eyes flew open. He shouldn't feel the sense of power he felt when Quinn took a step back, fear in her blue eyes, but he did. "Oh yeah, you go. You hurry off and forgot that I exist. I hope you enjoy it. My life. I hope that you remember that the only reason you're in that fucking car is because I nearly died!"

Quinn's eyes teared up and she opened her mouth but Luke wasn't done. "I bet you're really happy now. New offer of a contract for next year. Number two in the team while me, the person who helped make the team a success gets an I'm sorry visit from the boss because she's afraid of losing her girl racer. Whatcha do, Quinn? Throw around some hints that other teams were interested so Charlie would be forced to keep you in *my* car?"

Quinn's eyes widened. "Jesus, Luke. Is that what you think of me? After all we've been through? I'm well aware the reason I'm in the car is because of what happened to you, I know that." With her hand on her heart, Quin continued. "I struggled with it, getting in the car. I would have given anything for it to be you in there. I would never, ever wish you were hurt so I could drive the car. How could you think that? I love you."

Luke scoffed, tears blurring his vision. "Love me? Well, that's okay then. All's forgiven. You head off now so you don't miss your flight. Go and celebrate with your boyfriend and your groupies and all the fans who fawn over you. I hope that you are happy, Quinn. And hey, looks like Charlie should make it a multi-year deal because apparently, my progress is good, but not good enough. I'm done. I'm finished. My fucking life is over."

And then Luke lurched forward, trying to get away from Quinn and this shitshow but he fumbled, slamming hard against the wall, and pain radiated from his side causing him to let lose a groan of pain before his legs went from under him and he slumped down on the ground, his walker coming down on top of him.

"Jesus Christ, Luke, let me help you."

"I don't want your fucking help!" He shouted, grabbing his walker and throwing it, the apparatus hitting his bed with an unmerciful bang. He clenched his fists and beat them against his temple. "Just leave me alone. Leave me alone. I wish I'd never bloody woken up."

"Don't say that, Luke. Please don't say that." Quinn begged him but he just couldn't stand to look at her.

The admission seemed to flip a switch in him, and all the fight left his body. This was a nightmare, one he couldn't wake up from. This was how it was going to be from here on out, this empty feeling of nothingness and a chasm of loneliness.

"Just go, Quinn. Just leave me the hell alone."

Quinn hesitated making Luke yell at her to go again and she did, leaving him by himself but as he cradled his head in his hands and sobbed, he felt her watching him. Luke pulled his knees to his chest, crying out in frustration and when he had no more tears to cry, Luke sat in the dark for hours and he felt absolutely numb.

No, that was a lie.

He felt unravelled. He felt like he was back in the car and rolling and rolling, being crushed under the weight of the carbon fibre but this time, there was no oblivion at the end, and oh, how he craved that oblivion.

He was tired of fighting. He was tired of existing, and he was tired of the world and the way it seemed to have a knack for kicking him when he was down.

CHAPTER FOURTEEN

Emil

EMIL FROZE, unsure of what to say and to start, he laughed it off and pretended he did not understand what Alma was speaking of. But Oskar knew him, knew when he was keeping something from him and his friend glared at him with that sternness that had made grown men flinch.

"Your mother was the best confidant." Emil started, pulling his knees to his chest and resting his chin on them and Oskar released his shoulder. "I asked her once, if what I'm about to share with you, changed how she saw me and Alma, she said that there was that to her, and to you, I would always be Emil and nothing could change the pieces of your hearts that I occupied."

"Whatever could you have to say to me that you feel I would not understand? I did not understand my mother and I need to know what you felt you couldn't share with me."

Emil ran a hand roughly through his hair. "I did not mean to keep that part of myself from you but I was rather afraid that this part of me might disappoint you or make you think....less of me."

"Am I such a bastard?" Oskar asked with a serious expression on his face,

Chuckling softly at Oskar's clipped tone, well used to his often brisk nature. "No, it was because you were my best friend, my brother, the person I looked up to, and even as a young boy, I was always terrified that I would disappoint you."

"Well," Oskar began, a slight twinkle of amusement in his eyes, "Considering I am taller, you often had to look up to me."

Emil could do nothing but laugh at Oskar's attempt to ease the tension and Emil knew, that if he wanted to get out of the feeling of being stuck and unable to move forward with his life in the way that he wanted, he had to be honest with Oskar. It was not that he wanted to be the poster boy for any movement, he wasn't about to go public in a flamboyant fashion but perhaps finally being just himself might be enough.

"Come now, Emil. Tell me what has you thinking too hard."

It would be easier to shy away from things, to go back to how things were. However, Emil had come from nothing, had never backed down from something just because it was hard. Even if this felt like a defining moment in his life.

"It was not something I think I intentionally kept from you, I believe, nor am I ashamed of it or consider it a big deal." Emil rubbed the sweat on his palms off his jeans. "I like women. But I also like men."

If Oskar was surprised or shocked, he did not show it just merely pressed his lips together and waited for Emil to tell him more. It took Emil a few seconds before he felt able to continue.

"I have never thought of my sexuality in the form of labels. I think these days, we put too many labels upon ourselves and it is quite suffocating. I am attracted to men and women, I am attracted to people and maybe it is me being bisexual or, I believe the young ones these days might call it pansexual. However, I am just me, the same Emil, that has not changed."

Emil shrugged, feeling the weight of his friend's stare, and even though this was not a hard conversation to have, although it had been far easier than he had anticipation, Emil could not deny that he did indeed feel unburdened.

Oskar scratched at his blond stubble, moistening

his lips as he readied to speak. "I should have known, really." Oskar mused and his tone held a hint of amusement.

"Why is that oh wise one?"

Oskar's cool blue eyes slid to hold his as he said in a deadpan tone and an expressionless face. "You've been calling me a handsome bastard for years."

Emil almost choked as laughter bubbled from his lips as Oskar reached over and patted his arm. Oskar was smiling at him, yet his eyes seemed a little guarded as Emile said. "Your Quinn has done you good, my friend. I think they will start to call you the sarcastic sadist in the future instead of the silent one."

When Oskar had first turned up at Rebel Racers, Quinn had started calling him the silent sadist because of his no-nonsense attitude and limited speaking but Oskar had taken it all in his stride, and even now, he laughed along with Emil until they both halted and Oskar looked at him.

"You should have told me sooner, I wish you had told me sooner"

"If there was one person in this world I was afraid of rejecting me, it was you, Oskar. Even though I think I knew in my heart you would not, I was still afraid that there was a slim chance you might."

"I would not care who you dated," Oskar reassured him. "I would not have cared once they made you happy. But if they hurt you, man or woman, I would not be best pleased."

Emil embraced his friend, happy that now there was no secrets between them. when they finally broke apart, Oskar skimmed another rock across the water.

"Why now? What has happened to make you want to tell me? Have you met someone?"

Emil sighed, unsure of how to answer but since he was being honest, he decided to just get it all out in the open. "Maybe, I am not sure of what is happening at the moment but I fear that any feelings I may have, or that he may have, are destined to cause pain to both of us."

Oskar was contemplative for a moment before it seemed to dawn on him. "Ahh, Luke. You two have gotten close?"

"You could say that." Emil chuckled, ribbing the back of his neck, feeling flush. "Can I admit it does feel a little strange to be speaking to you about a boy I like?"

"Sure it is, but I am glad that you are now. You can always come to me. You can always talk to me."

Oskar had that no-nonsense tone that Emil knew better than to argue with him.

"Luke is in a difficult place right now, and I, I am realizing that it would be nice to have my very own Quinn in my life."

"I'm afraid Quinn is taken," Oskar said with a smug smirk and Emil rolled his eyes before he continued.

"There is a spark. A connection between us. He

kissed me the other night after you called and I hadn't expected it and he mistook that for me being appalled that he kissed me and I cannot get him to stay in the room long enough to assure him that I had in fact liked being kissed by him. and I am acutely aware that this might be too much information after I just came out to you."

Oskar skimmed another stone along the water. "I had the same issue with Quinn."

Emil lifted his brows and Oskar chuckled. "Well, a similar issue. A misunderstanding of sorts. But it was only after we saw you in Dublin and you talked some sense into me that I acted on the attraction. Quinn assumed that when I was reluctant to kiss her that it was because I saw her as less than, and perhaps Luke, who has kept this massive part of himself so caged doesn't know how to act on his attraction."

Emil clasped his friend's shoulder. "I do give great advice. I will be sure to brag more often about all my sage advice that propelled you on the path to your true love."

Oskar snorted, shaking his head. "If you and Luke get your act together, you may beat us to the altar, my friend."

The thought of having that kind of future never seemed possible to Emil but now that Oskar had said it, Emil had to admit that being someone's husband sounded like something he might aspire to. Oskar grinned as Emil felt a blush heat his face.

Oskar's phone rang before Emil had a chance to say another word and from the goofy smile that curved Oskar's lips, it could only be one person.

"Quinn," Oskar said into the phone his grin falling from his face. "Woah, slow down, Quinn. I can't understand you. Explain it to me slowly. What happened with Luke?"

Oskar got to his feet and grabbed his mother's urn and inclined his head toward the car as Emil followed after him, waiting with his heart racing as he heard Oskar tell Quinn they were on the way back and would meet her at the apartment.

Oskar obviously had learned a thing or two from his girl racer because he took off at breakneck speed and Emil listened in horror as Oskar explained what had happened and Emil's heart almost broke as Oskar explained what had happened between Luke and Quinn.

CHAPTER FIFTEEN

Luke

HE DAYS PASSED by but Luke wasn't keeping track of them. He had decided that he had had enough and was done with it all. He simply stopped. Luke stopped going to physio, and didn't bother going to his counselling sessions. His phone had been switched off after his blow out with Quinn and he kept his room door closed.

Luke had tried to check himself out but the doctors reminded him he was contractually obligated to stay as mandated by Rebel Racers. He wasn't sure why he didn't just walk about because he was done fighting for something that probably was going to be ripped from his grasp and yet, he stayed, that tiny little shred of hope that his world wasn't completely over.

Emil had come by to knock at his door several times but Luke had ignored him. He pretended to be sleeping or when he was just done pretending, Luke just blatantly ignored him. He wasn't sure he could deal with the rejection after everything else over the last few days.

The only thing he managed to drag himself to was a check-up where they told him the inflammation had gone down slightly in his hip and that was a good sign. Luke wasn't so sure he believed it. His hip had been paining him since his fall, the nurses having rushed him for a scan after Quinn had told him that he had fallen, and he wasn't any more damaged than he already was, but then again, he hadn't done anything to try and get back on his feet. At this stage, he really didn't see the point.

The monotonous routine of using the walker and striding from one side of the room to the other had frustrated Luke so the walker had sat idle for many an hour as Luke perched himself on one of the seats and looked out over the city.

If life had been fair, tonight he would be getting ready for the first practice session of the next day and the adrenaline would be immense. His routine usually consisted of an early dinner, a quick workout, and a strategy session before getting a good night's sleep if he could.

And Luke had been thinking a lot about his road to F1. It had all started when his dad had built a kart with him when he was probably about seven and they had worked night and day to finish it. Then Luke had learned how to drive it, down hills and around carparks, pedalling as fast as his little legs would let him. He had loved every moment of it.

Mick had taken him to a local karting track and the smell of oil and petrol clung to his skin for days after. It had come to him so easily, the karting, and he'd won a few little competitions. Then he had gone to an open day for Philip Coyle's new racetrack. Philip had been impressed with Luke's knowledge and skills. He told him about his plans, in time, to start his own racing team and try and get into F1.

Luke had been an F1 fan for years, watching every race weekend with his dad, and even when Mick was working, F1 Sundays for race day was a tradition. He had watched when Fernando Alonso ended Michael Schumacher's dominance to become the youngest F1 champion. He had witnessed Sebastian Vettel's dominance until the new era was ushered in.

Luke had watched for years and years and dreamt of taking the top step of the podium and then, working his ass off so that his name was added to the long list of world champions. He knew even when he had to attend school that all he ever really wanted to do was drive. He had done enough to pass his leaving cert, but all that he had learned had been expunged from his brain to make way for all the intrinsic details needed to drive in the best sport in the world.

When Philip had approached Luke when he was eighteen and asked him if he was willing to put in the time and effort to fight for the chance to race in F1. Luke had jumped at the chance. While his parents weren't struggling for money, they had no means to back Luke in his dream to become a champion driver but Philip had.

For years Luke had eaten, slept, drank, and breathed racing. He had trained his body and mind to be that of a champion. Philip had gotten him sponsorship deals and backing and then they had the chance to get into F1 when one of the race teams went bankrupt and Philip seized his opportunity.

Noah had been an immediate hit with the F1 world; the boy who came from nothing to join the world's most expensive sport. But Noah had no time for the media and that intrigued them more. The women flocked around him, hoping to tame the brooding driver even though Luke knew that Noah was waiting for the girl he loved to come back to him.

Luke knew he wasn't ugly, knew that he was somewhat attractive but the world started to talk when Luke showed up to events alone, when he had no chemistry with the models in photoshoots. For some reason, drenched in his melancholy, he was reminded of a conversation he had with Philip after a magazine

interview asked him some personal questions and he
had walked out embarrassed.

"You wanna tell me what happened today, son?"

*Luke lifted his gaze to Philip and for some reason,
this felt as hard as coming out to his parents. He hadn't
told anyone in his team that he was gay. It wasn't that
he was trying to hide it, but the conversation around his
sexuality hadn't come up.*

*"I know Noah has this thing about shoots with
models and the like but you've always been okay with it?
Is there a reason why today was the day you channelled
your hot-headed teammate and lost your cool? That's not
like you, Luke."*

*Philip was right about it not being like him. Noah
was the fiery one and Luke was the smiley cheerful one
who loved taking pictures with fans and signing autographs. Noah had no issues chatting to younger fans, to
families but he never had any time for the scantily clad
women who knew nothing about the sport but just
wanted to bed a racer car driver.*

*"I'm sorry, Philip. I'll call the interviewer and apol-
ogize. I lost my temper. He just kept asking personal
questions and it annoyed me."*

*Philip leaned forward in his seat and regarded
Luke. "We can mitigate any unwanted personal questions. I'll set up a few "dates" with a model or two that
will end because of conflicting work schedules. That
should take the focus off you."*

"I don't think that will help," Luke admitted,

running his fingers through his hair as Philip waited for him to continue. "The paps will take photos and just like before, realize that it's all fake and a photo opportunity. That's all it ever will be."

Luke swallowed hard, then lowered his gaze. "Philip, I'm gay"

There was this gaping silence, then Philip cleared his throat. "Well, that explains it then. I'm guessing you're not out then?"

"My family knows. Noah doesn't."

"Tell him," Philip ordered, but there was a softness in his tone. "Noah's a good kid, and you two need to be upfront with each other. Thanks for telling me, Luke. It changes nothing, if that's what stopped you from telling me before. I'll get a plan in place to promote you as this focused, driven, individual who doesn't want outside distractions to get in the way of F1. Unless you want me to help you tell the world."

Luke contemplated it for a moment. It would be easier and harder all at once to just come out to everyone but then he would never be just called an F1 champion; it would be the first gay f1 champion. The first gay pole sitter, the first gay race winner. The headlines would never simply read; Luke Sullivan Formula One champion of the world.

He didn't want to make any bold statements. He just wanted to win as himself.

So, Luke had declined Philips's offer and a week later, a fresh interview was published where Luke had explained that he felt it unfair to try and date when he was so focused on his career and that once he was world champion, then he might be able to relax enough to date.

Six years later and he felt like he had sacrificed a part of himself for absolutely nothing.

The door to the balcony opened and Emil ducked outside and Luke's heart stuttered. Before he even had a chance to utter a word, Emil closed the door and came towards him.

"This pity party needs to stop. You have got to fight. You will walk again and you need to snap out of this black hole you've gotten into. Get up and move your ass, Luke."

"Why? Why Should I?"

Emil's lips curved into a very kissable smile as those dark eyes of his filled with a heat Luke didn't understand. "You will get up off your ass and fight. But let me give you an incentive. The day you walk across a room without an aid and I promise to give you that blowjob you asked for the day we met."

CHAPTER SIXTEEN

Luke

"WALK ACROSS A ROOM without an aid and I promise to give you that blowjob you asked for the day we met."

Luke felt heat singe his cheeks even as his body hardened and if Emil kept looking at him with the hunger in his eyes, Luke might forget that there was no way in hell Emil meant what he was saying.

"I have no clue what you're on about." Luke managed to grind out, however, the flaming in his cheeks told Emil otherwise.

Emil grinned, coming forward to rest his hands on the armrest of the chair, blocking Luke in, and with him so close, Luke realized just how good Emil smelt and he wanted to bury his nose in the crook of his neck and just breathe him in.

"I suppose a blowjob is out of the question?" Emil repeated his words back to him, a devilish smile on his lips. "That is what you muttered before you turned an adorable shade of red. I wanted to lick your freckles there and then to see of your skin was as flush and hot as it looked."

Luke sucked in a breath, shaking his head. "You don't like men."

Emil chuckled then, leaning in a little more. "Then why did I just tell my best friend that I did? Why did I tell him that I was attracted to you?"

This wasn't happening, right? This was all a dream and he would wake up soon. Luke pinched his arm, felt the pain, and knew then that Emil was in fact admitting to being attracted to him.

"But you were horrified when I kissed you?"

Ugh, Luke hated how pathetic he sounded, especially when Emil retreated a little.

"I was grieving and confused. I had wanted to kiss you for some time but in the moment, I didn't expect it. You left before I could explain that on any other occasion, I would have welcomed the kiss."

"I made a mistake. I didn't mean to kiss you. It was a massive mistake and can never happen again. I think you should go."

"I certainly hope that is not true. I would very much like to fuck you."

Luke blushed harder and that made Emil chuckle

before he stepped back and gave Luke some breathing space.

"I think you like the idea of being fucked by me. Good."

Panic tried to quash down the lust surging through Luke. Over the past few months, his emotions had confused him but where Emil was concerned, he was certain that he had to know what it was like to be kissed by him, to be touched by him. Luke yearned to feel his muscles clench as Emil roamed his hands over his body and he wanted to see if his own touch could make Emil groan his name.

"I can see where your mind is going but if I give in now, if I give you what we both crave, then you have no incentive to get better. I am here to motivate you that there are things worth fighting for in this world and I assure you, my mouth is very talented. All of me is."

Luke didn't have a clue what was happening. He was flustered and taken aback by the bluntness of Emil's words. Luke had had very limited physical contact with other men, apart from a few drunken kisses, and from the way Emil was talking, he obviously had far more experience than him.

Despite the fact that he wanted Emil to prove just how talented his mouth was, Luke suddenly felt self-conscious. What if this was another feeble attempt to get him out of his funk?

"I don't need a pity fuck."

The words tumbled from Luke's lips before he could stop the errant thought from slipping from his brain out into the room. Emil's eyes darkened, and Luke knew he had insulted him. Luke got to his feet, turning away from Luke as he used the furniture to walk toward the wall and then lean against it.

"I can assure you, as you so delicately put it, it wouldn't be a pity fuck. I *want* you. You might not be used to having people be this honest with you, but what if I tell you that the last time I jerked off in the shower, it was your name on my lips, that it was your hand I imagined stroking me to madness? If you can tell me that the same can't be said for you, then I will walk out of this room and we shall never speak of it again."

It was on the tip of his tongue to deny it but thinking about Emil dripping wet in the shower, head bowed back as he came with Luke's name on his lips kept the words at bay, and from the very smug and satisfied look on Emil's face, he knew that Luke couldn't deny it.

"Or do you want a little taste of what can be, when you are strong enough to stand on your own two feet? Yes, perhaps that could be the best incentive."

Luke felt his heart stop as Emil strode over to him, and they stood face to face, almost the same height, but Emil stopped shy of pressing his lips to Luke's. Instead, Emil leaned in and pressed the lightest of kisses to

Luke's jaw while trailing a hand up Luke's arm, causing Luke to shiver.

Emil blazed a trail of kisses along his jaw, then Luke's neck, the kisses changing from a brief press of lips to wet, open-mouth kisses, and then Emil sucked on the curve where his neck and shoulders met and Luke threw back his head and moaned.

When Emil rocked his hips forward, their hardened cocks pressed against one another's and they both moaned this time. Luke brought his head back up to clash eyes with Emil as the other man slid one hand into Luke's hair and the other reached down to cup his erection through his jeans.

"Would you like me to stop?"

Was Emil crazy? Like hell Luke wanted him to stop. He wanted to strip Emil bare and marvel at the body he had admired from afar for too long. He wanted to taste his skin, drag his hands through Emil's hair, and let the world fade away.

"No, don't stop," Luke said, grabbing Emil by the tee in case he decided to torture him and leave him ready to combust. "Please don't bloody stop."

Luke watched the grin curve Emil's lips before Emil tugged his hair and Luke was a goner. Emil yanked him down for a kiss, and it was life-changing for Luke. There was no coyness in this kiss; it was demanding and possessive, Emil taking charge and as someone who was used to being in utter control of every aspect of his life, Luke felt even more turned on that Emil had clearly taken the leading role.

Emil's tongue tangled with his and Luke felt his hips l jerk forward into Emil's hand, then Emil sucked on his bottom lip, holding it between his teeth before he captured Luke's mouth with his own again. Time stood still as Luke wrapped his arms around Emil, wanting to pull him closer and closer. Hands roamed freely, as Emil continued to use that talented mouth on him.

It was only when Luke reached down and popped the button of Emil's jeans did the other man pull his mouth from Luke's and grab his hands. "Ah ah, No more until after you get your sea legs back."

Luke's lips felt swollen from the kissing and the adrenaline surging in his bones made him feel brave, and his face was flush enough to hide the blush as Luke grinned. "That was for the blowjob. Are you telling me that a handjob is out of the question? I can do that sitting down. My hands work grand."

Emil grinned, rolling his eyes, winking at Luke. "Nope. And do not try and tempt me. We have struck a deal, you and I, this night. What wretched torturous foreplay it will be for both of us the longer it takes you to walk across the room under your own steam and tell me to get on my knees."

Luke groaned with frustration. "Are you trying to kill me? I'm not sure I have many lives left."

The chuckle that came from Emil was dark and

seductive. "Enough of that for tonight. Let us order some unhealthy food and perhaps, if you are very good, we can watch a movie and make out some more."

Luke laughed, shaking his head as Emil ordered food to be delivered and after, as they lay side by side in the bed watching a movie, their finger interlocked, Luke began to feel like he could fight again.

But what would happen when they left the bubble of the rehab facility and stepped back into the normal world? Luke wasn't sure if he was ready to walk down a street holding another man's hand, even if that man was Emil.

Emil leaned in and kissed his jawline then, and Luke decided those were worries for another day.

CHAPTER SEVENTEEN

Emil

HE CHANGE in Luke had been instantaneous.

The following morning after their make-out session and having fallen asleep together, waking up in a tangle of limbs, Emil had seen doubt creep over Luke's face so he'd kissed him, morning breath and all.

They had separated in order to shower and when Emil went to go find Luke, he was delighted to see him back in the gym with Mark the physio. Emil had left him to it, sneaking off to the garden to kick around his football.

Technically, Emil had been given the go-ahead to head back to Denmark to begin training with the squad but he had asked for another few weeks' respite. He had never taken any time off since he joined the squad so the team were happy to give it to him.

A couple of weeks passed by and Luke and he had
fallen into a routine. Every night, they came together
to watch movies, or simply spend time getting to know
one another before lots of serious making out that had
Emil contemplating breaking his vow and giving in to
Luke, especially when he tempted him by cupping his
straining erection.

They had gotten more hot and heavy over the
time, and last night, Luke had stripped him of his tee
and Emil had rolled on top of Luke and it had been
rather difficult to put the brakes on what was
happening between them, even as Emil rolled off Luke
and lay looking at the ceiling with a groan of frustration.

Luke was back in the gym this morning so Emil
had gone back out into the garden, forgoing the
specialized training facilities, and went back to his
roots, just him, the open air, and the ball, and began to
kick the ball against the wall. It was familiar to him,
running from spot to spot to keep the ball in motion
and while he might not be able to properly train, this
was the closest he could get.

"Emil, spark den til mig."

Emil turned as the ball came to his foot and he
kicked it up to his knee and then grinned as he did as
Oskar had asked and kicked the ball to him. Oskar
might not be a professional footballer, but he had
spent years working and training with the Danish
squad. And even before that, poor Oskar had been

forced to spend an hour kicking a ball around with him whenever they had a free moment.

Oskar easily stopped the ball and flicked it up with his foot a few times before kicking it back to Emil with a grin. Quinn on the other hand was rolling her eyes, tension in her shoulders as she glanced over her shoulders, and Emil knew that she was afraid of bumping into Luke.

The racer was holding a basket, looking from Emil to Oskar as they kicked the ball around until Emil rushed forward, moving like lightning on his feet, and turned at the last minute, edging the ball around Oskar and kicking it against the wall and essentially scoring a goal.

Oskar was laughing as he rolled up the sleeves of his shirt. "We were back for a couple of days and I wanted to come see you. I brought food."

The weather was nice enough to sit outside so they commandeered one of the outdoor picnic tables and Emil studied the couple as they worked in sync to lay out all the food and the drinks on the table without looking at one another. They seemed so in tune with one another that it made Emil crave that for himself, and when Quinn reached over and handed Oskar sunscreen, Oskar glared at Quinn even as his lips twitched.

When Oskar had gone to Australia, he had a reaction to the sun that had made him delirious and as the sun shone uncharacteristically warm today, it looked like Quinn was taking no chances in Oskar getting sick again.

Oskar had spent so much time looking after everyone else, it was quite heart-warming to see someone looking after Oskar.

"Quinn, it's not even that warm. I'll be grand." Oskar said the last part in a sort of not-Irish accent.

Emil almost chuckled at Oskar's attempts at an Irish accent, but Quinn looked at him sideways with a no-nonsense expression. "I'm not taking any chances. When we were in Denmark and it was Baltic you told me to wear the snow boots when we were out and about and I listened because I like my feet."

Oskar swooped in and kissed her cheek. "I quite like your feet too."

"That is too much information." Emil sighed as he rolled his eyes and ate some crisps from the package Quinn had just opened.

Oskar and Quinn both laughed, then sat down and they ate and chatted away for a time. There was nothing heavy about the conversation. Emil noticed Oskar stealing glances at him occasionally as if he was concerned for him and in the end, Emil sat back in his seat.

"Spit it out, Oskar. Tell me what has you fussing about like a mother hen." Emil told him, watching as Oskar glanced at Quinn which made Emil raise his brows even more. "You haven't told her?"

Quinn wasn't even looking at either of them as Oskar replied. "It was not my secret to tell."

A snort escaped Quinn's nose as they both turned to look at her. The girl grinned then shrugged. "You mean that Emil and a certain redhead are kinda flirting with one another? Oh nah, I knew all along."

Oskar looked stunned by Emil just laughed. "Perhaps you should have been a detective."

"Nope. Happy with the job I have, thanks. Besides, when he's not being a stupid idiot, Luke's kinda awesome. If getting his head out of his ass means him getting naked and sweaty with a certain Danish footballer, then I'm all for it."

If Emil hadn't already loved his best friend's girlfriend, then that statement would have done it for him. It mattered not to Quinn who he was, just that Emil could make Luke happy. He wished that the world was full of Quinn Murphy's so that maybe Luke and in truth, himself, hadn't felt the need to keep a vital part of himself hidden.

"You didn't say a thing to me about what you knew."

Quinn shrugged, tucking a strand of blue-black hair behind her ear. "As you said, it wasn't my secret to share. I love Luke. I just want him to be happy." Quinn lifted her eyes to Emil. "I'm kinda fond of you too, Emil. But if you break his heart, you won't see me coming."

Emil put a hand on his heart and feigned shock. "And if he breaks my heart."

"Then Oskar can have a word. He's my brother. I got his back."

They all laughed and that was the matter closed. They chatted about plans for the rest of the year, with October and November not too far away and Quinn invited Emil to an upcoming charity event that Rebel Racers was hosting to raise money for underprivileged youths to get into motorsport.

Emil gladly accepted knowing he could fly back between Euro qualifiers to attend if there was no game that weekend. It would be good publicity and an excuse for him to see Luke.

That made him smile as Oskar began to tell him about his and Quinn's plans to buy or build a house to make Ireland their permanent home, with Oskar wanting a minimalistic home that Quinn called a Danish home, and Quinn wanting a room with her own driving simulator. It was hilarious at the role reversals, with Quinn essentially wanting a man cave and Oskar wanting open spaces.

They both glared at him when Emil shared with them his thoughts on the matter, which only made Emil laugh harder. Emil hadn't known just how much he needed this respite, how much he missed his friend and being able to share a meal like they had most weeks in London.

"Emil? Are you out here?"

Emil froze at the sound of Luke's voice, his eyes darting to Quinn, who had also stiffened. Turning his head, Emil saw Luke walk slowly toward them, no longer using the walker but using two canes to help him move with a silly grin that fell the moment he saw Emil dining with Quinn and Oskar.

"Shit, I'm sorry." Luke looked crestfallen. "I didn't mean to interrupt. I'll go."

Emil was torn about what to do next. Part of him wanted to go to Luke because it was an achievement to see him standing without the aid of the walker but the argument was between Luke and Quinn and it was not his place to invite Luke to join them, just in case it made Quinn uncomfortable.

"Don't go," Quinn said, lifting her gaze to smile at Luke before reaching into her basket and taking out a container she had left in there. "I gotcha some of those noodles you like. Their probably cold now, but that never stopped you before."

Chapter Eighteen

Luke

LUKE SWALLOWED down his shame and flashed Quinn a grin. "I could eat. Once you didn't cook them that is. I don't think I ever recovered from the time you tried to cook a roast and it was still raw when you served it up to us."

Quinn laughed as she set the container of noodles down next to Emil. "How was I supposed to know that you couldn't cook it from frozen?"

"It was on the bloody instructions."

"Everyone's a goddamn critic," Quinn mumbled, rolling her eyes. "Sit your skinny ass down before I decided to be mean and not share food."

Luke was still adjusting to walking with the

canes instead of the walker but his movements had gotten more stable on the walk from the gym. Mark had been pleased with his progress and the inflammation had died down so he was another step closer to being cane free and getting his hands on Emil.

As Luke set the canes against the wall, he slipped into the seat beside Emil, glancing at him when the other man slid a hand along his thigh and squeezed his knee in support.

Quinn handed him a fork, and Luke offered his thanks and then Quinn asked Luke if he had heard about Jameson's new girlfriend and the drama surrounding them. Jameson Kent was Luna's bandmate, a man who had lost his girlfriend in a hit and run. He was a quiet man who walked with a heaviness in his shoulders so Luke listened as Quinn filled him in on all the gossip.

The chatter was friendly enough as Luke ate his noodles, knowing that he needed to clear the air with Quinn and mend any broken fences his breakdown might have ruined. He and Quinn always had an easy relationship, one that was built on trust and love, and he would hate to think that he might have ripped that apart because he felt like his own world was crumbling around the.

The sun went in quickly and Luke shivered, his shorts and t-shirt not much defence against the cold wind that was sweeping through the garden. The only two that weren't shivering were the men born in a country that had frequent snow.

"Hey, I'm cold. I'm gonna head in and get a hoodie. Quinn, wanna walk me back and you can borrow one of mine?"

It pained him to see a reluctance in her eyes before she nodded. "Sure, It'll give the Eskimos a few minutes to chat."

Luke slid his legs out from under the table and grabbed his canes, getting to his feet much easier now as he waited as Quinn kissed Oskar's cheek, the man's lips curving into a small smile, then his glacier blue eyes slid to Luke and he nodded once, and Luke couldn't tell if he was warning him against hurting Quinn or Emil.

Maybe it was both.

Luke walked ahead as Quinn spoke with Oskar for a few minutes and in a quick few strides, she had caught up to him and fallen into step with him. They didn't say anything as they walked inside where it was warmer so Luke waited until they were in the elevator before he started speaking.

"Hey Quinn, I'm sorry," He began, resting his hip against the wall of the elevator. "It's not an excuse but when you showed up, Charlie had just told me she was dropping me next year and then I had the inflammation in my hip. And other stuff... If you had showed up a day or two later, I could have handled it better. I wouldn't have been so angry."

It was a half-truth, because the person Luke was really angry with was himself for not being stronger, for not getting fitter faster.

They walked back to his room before Quinn perched herself on the end of his bed and leaned back on her hands. "I didn't know about Charlie when I came that day. Honestly, I didn't. If I'd known then I'd have stayed away. I told Charlie it was wrong to tell you first. It was wrong to count you out because I know that I'm on borrowed time in the seat. I know you're coming back for it and the offers from other teams were because I didn't want to go back to not racing."

Quinn sounded so sure that Luke was going to come back and as someone who was currently in a position where he would not be in the car anytime soon, he understood why Quinn had been entertaining offers from other teams.

"Quinn," Luke said softly as he slipped his arms into a hoody he grabbed from a chair by the door before he sat down. "you do know there's a really big chance I won't ever get in the car again. Stay with Rebel Racers. I would prefer it be you in the car, working with Noah, if it can't be me. And once I'm able to walk about without the canes, I'll be back on track to cheer you on."

Quinn's eyes brimmed with tears. "God Luke, when you crashed, I couldn't breathe and no one would show me what happened until days later but seeing you in that hospital bed, seeing you so still, it broke me."

Tears slipped out of her eyes and slipped down her cheeks and Luke only then realized how hard it must have been for his family and friends when they didn't know if he would wake up. There was a long list of drivers who weren't so lucky, who never woke up.

Luke didn't know if he could stand to embrace Quinn just yet. "Hey come here."

Quinn slid off the bed and threw herself at him, burying her face in his shoulder and Luke, and Luke wrapped his arms around her and held her, even as she crawled into his lap and Luke stroked her hair.

"I hope Oskar is firm in his knowledge that I'm gay or else he's not gonna be best pleased that I'm holding you."

Quinn laughed, lifting her head and swiping at her eyes. "Oskar knows how much I love my older, slightly infuriating brothers. And I do love you, Luke."

"I love you too, small fry."

"I'm not hurting you am I?"

"Nope, all good. Must be making progress."

"Enough to have your wicked way with Emil?" Quinn teased, her laughter filling the room when Luke felt his cheeks burn. "Or have you guys already done it?"

"No, but not for the lack of wanting to. He's being really firm on stance to have me when I can stand on my own two feet."

"Huh," Quinn mused as she got to her feet. "sex as motivation. May need to steal that and square it away for future reference."

Luke barked out a laugh, rolling his eyes. "Poor Oskar and to think we once thought he was all silent and sadistic. Didn't you once tell him you'd seen more passion in a block of ice?"

"Well, he's disproved that on numerous occasions, let me tell ya."

"Quinn!"

His friend shrugged and grinned. "I'm sorry, I thought we were sharing about my fabulous sex life and the fact your very own sexy Viking hasn't put out yet?"

Luke sighed. "You're terrible."

"I know," Quinn responded with a shrug. Then she looked at him. "Luke, promise me that you won't try and sabotage what you have with Emil because you're frightened. Noah did it with Charlie and I sure as shit almost blew it with Oskar because I was terrified. Emil is a good man and I think he and you could be good together. Please, Luke."

Luke heard himself promise Quinn that he would try but it felt like a lie to him. Being with Emil in the safety of the facility, away from the public eye, made it so much easier to act on his feelings and yet, he didn't know if it was in him to sit down to dinner in a restaurant and hold Emil's hand across the table.

But for now he could dream that he and Emil lived

normal lives that didn't involve the press or the media, where he wasn't an injured F1 driver and Emil wasn't one of the most loved footballers in Denmark and the world, where dealing with the public was inevitable.

Oskar and Emil appeared at the door and it saved Luke from having to answer any more serious questions. Luke pulled Quinn into a hug, asking her if they were good and Quinn told him that they were, and she would bring Noah the next time she came to see him.

"Go and give um hell on the racetrack, Quinn," Luke said, giving her a bright smile even though he felt sad that it wasn't him getting ready for the final racers of the season.

"I love you, big bro."

Luke put his hand over his heart. "I love you too, little sis. I love you too."

CHAPTER NINETEEN

Luke

LUKE HAD TRIED to follow Quinn's wise words, enjoying his time with Emil, and working hard to get to walking on his own. It had taken another couple of weeks, but a few days ago, Luke had walked the length and breadth of the gym without needing his canes or experiencing any pain. Mark, his physio, had been so delighted he had hugged him and lifted Luke off his feet.

It made him feel like he had achieved something fantastic. But he hadn't told Emil just yet. Not that Luke was avoiding getting intimate with Emil, though considering his lack of experience, it should be something for him to worry about. He wanted to surprise him and since Luke had been signed off on losing the canes, Emil had been busy in meetings all week. That was Luke's excuse anyway and he was sticking with it.

The anticipation had almost done his head in. It had taken all of his control when Emil had slipped into his bed not to scream from the top of his lungs that he had been cleared. Then Emil had kissed him and Luke forgot all about walking.

Today, he'd had a very good video call with Charlie. It had been hard for him to speak to her, especially when he had blamed her a little for giving up on him. Charlie herself had been expressionless when the call started but when Luke apologized for his behaviour, her face had crumbled.

"Luke," Charlie had sighed. "There's no need for apologies. I should have handled it better. I panicked, having to give bad news to a friend and I should have waited. I did a piss poor job as your boss and as your friend."

Luke had assured her that at any time being told he was being sidelined for at least a year would have killed him and he had other stuff going on in his personal life that had been the catalyst for his anger at the time.

Charlie asked if there was anything she could do to support him, and Luke told her that for now, he was grand, but maybe in the future. She had smiled at that, then glanced at something on her desk before she chewed on her lip like she was struggling to know if she should say what she wanted to say.

She had laughed when Luke told her to spit it out.

"Listen, I'm probably going to put my foot in it and now we've cleared the air, I don't want to upset you again but, since you'll still be a member of this family, and since you're on your feet again, how about you come and be part of our strategic team? It would be great to have someone in the room for some of those meetings that knows what it's like to drive the car."

"I dunno, Charlie." Luke had replied, not sure if he could be at the track and not get in the car and if that would be weird for him.

"Don't answer me now. We've got time. But I know Noah misses having you there at race weekends, and so does Quinn."

Luke had laughed then, stating he was sure that Charlie and Oskar kept them busy, but Charlie had dismissed him with a wave of her hand saying it wasn't the same. "He wanted to do this adventure day the other week and while I love a good adrenaline rush, I wasn't keen on climbing down a mountain. His response was that Luke would have been well up for it."

Luke had laughed but did say that if his parents found out that he had gone leaping off the side of a cliff, so soon after nearly dying, they'd kill him first and then Noah.

But it had given him a case of the warm and fuzzies.

Emil told him to come by around nine after his

zoom call so Luke had showered, then used the canes to cross the room and knocked at the door before he opened it. Just putting away his laptop, Emil was naked from the waist up, giving Luke a delicious view of his well-defined abs and the v that dipped down.. He wore a loose pair of shorts and his lips curved into a smile.

"Hello, gorgeous."

Luke flushed and that made Emil smile even more. "I've been thinking about you all day."

Emil rose from the chair and came over to brush his lips against Luke's. Setting the canes over to the side, Luke took Emil's face in his hands and kissed him hard on the mouth. Against his lips, Luke felt the vibration of Emil's chuckle as Luke stepped back and traced his palms over Emil's shoulders, down his chest, and along his rib cage.

"You're in a playful mood this evening." Emil mused, and Luke revelled in the way his taunt stomach muscles clenched as Luke caressed his chest.

And Luke was feeling playful, leaning down, Luke pressed an open mouth kiss to Emil's pec, flicking his tongue over a nipple and that made Emil moan, the sound egging him on.

"Luke, gods, you're trying to kill me."

Luke switched to the other side and sucked on Emi's neglected nipple. "Maybe. Or maybe I'm trying to convince you that we've been very good at waiting but I don't want to wait anymore. I don't want to waste any more time waiting."

Putting his hands on Emil's hips, Luke straightened, pulling Emil flush against him, and the rock hardness of his cock pressed against his, and this time, Luke shuddered. Slipping his hands round he cupped Emil's ass and Emil laughed. "Definitely playful."

Luke continued to tease Emil, trailing his lips along his collarbone, as he rocked his hips, delighted that there was no pain or stiffness. Emil must have been as affected by the foreplay as he was because he dragged Luke away from kissing his shoulder and back to his lips.

Their mouths collided, the passion that had been present since the first proper kiss still igniting Luke's blood as they vented their sexual frustration in a kiss that was all tongue and teeth.

This time, it was Emil who broke the kiss and stalked away, walking to the window and grabbing a bottle of water that he must have had while on his calls. He was breathing hard, as was Luke, and in those dark brown eyes, Luke could almost see the struggle in him.

Luke yanked his own tee over his head and tossed it aside, Emil's eyes hungrily drinking him in and Luke was glad that he had been able to get his body back in shape to see Emil watching him.

"Come back over here and kiss me," Luke said, grinning when Emil shook his head.

"I do not think that's a good idea."

This was it. This was what Luke had been waiting all week for and now that it was here, his palms were sweaty, but Luke knew life was short and tomorrow wasn't granted, so he didn't want to live any more of his life not being happy.

"I think it's a great idea." Luke teased, letting his own hand slip down and cup his erection. It gave him a spike of adrenaline and it reminded him of the feeling he got driving down a long straight on the racetrack and braking late into the corner.

"I think it's a great idea," Luke said again, licking his lips before he continued. "Or maybe I should walk over and kiss you."

Taking a deep breath and steeling himself against the possibility that he could land on his ass, or stumble and kill the mood he had been trying to build since he walked into the room. Then Luke put one foot in front of the other, Emil's eyes widening in surprise as Luke crossed the floor, just stopping short of where Emil stood, mouth open.

"When? When did this happen?"

The sound of pure joy in Emil's tone made Luke want to kiss him again and he would, as soon as possible.

"A couple of days ago. Mark signed off that I could lose the canes and I wanted to surprise you but you've been busy all week. Honestly, though I wanted to make sure I didn't embarrass myself when I was trying hard to seduce you. Face planting would not be sexy at all when you're trying to divest a lover of his clothes."

Emil dragged him into a hug and Luke wrapped his arms around Emil's back. "I am so so happy for you. This is amazing, Luke. Truly amazing!"

Releasing him, Emil kissed the side of his mouth, then his eyes twinkled with mischief. "I guess you'll be wanting me to live up to my end of the bargain."

"Eventually," Luke grinned, taking a step back, and then he went to the door and turned the lock to make sure they weren't disturbed. "I think, for now, I'd like to get my hands on that gorgeous body of yours. And maybe my lips. I want to be with you. In every way possible."

CHAPTER TWENTY

Emil

EMIL HAD BEEN WANTING to get Luke naked for a long time and the thought that it was finally happening. Luke lingered in the doorway, heat in his eyes but also a vulnerability, the blush on his cheeks endearing. Emil sensed the sudden change in his bravado, so Emil strode over to where he stood at the door, crowding Luke, but Emil didn't lean in and capture Luke's mouth like he wanted to.

Luke's breath hitched, his hands coming up to cup the side of Emil's neck. It was Luke who leaned forward to gently, almost hesitantly press his lips to Emil's. The kiss started slow, a press of lips, a nip to the bottom lip, and then Luke swept his tongue along the seam of Emil's lips, and the moment Emil's lips parted, Luke devoured his mouth, plunging his tongue in and out as if he was starved for Emil.

When the kiss broke, Emil took charge, setting the pace and making up for lost time. His hands touched Luke's ribs, and Luke's abs bunched under his touch. Sliding his hands up Luke's torso, he traced the plains of his chest, his shoulders, down his arms before he ducked his head and pressed an open-mouth kiss to Luke's pecs.

Luke hissed at the contact, Emil smiling against Luke's heated skin, flicking his tongue over his nipple. The moan that almost purred from Luke made Emil's already hardened cock throb.

as Luke ogled him. Fingers moving to the strings on Luke's grey joggers, Emil stripped Luke down to his boxers, taking time to seduce him as he removed his clothes, dragging his hands down over Luke's firm buttocks, pausing so Luke could kick off his shoes and then get rid of his trousers.

The evidence of Luke's erection was clear, his bulge making Emil lick his lips. He knew Luke said that he should wait to suck him off but Emil wanted to taste him, to take Luke's cock into his mouth and suck and lick until Luke was trembling with his release.

Emil yanked down Luke's boxers, freeing his pulsing cock, and dropped to his knees in front of Luke.

"Emil, I don't think I can stay upright if you do that."

Lifting his gaze, Emil grinned, sliding his hands up Luke's thighs, keeping one hand firmly on his thigh and then Emil wrapped his hand around Luke's thick hard, length and stroked. Luke cursed, his head kicking back, his legs quivering. Emil glanced up at Luke, making sure he was okay, asking him if he was okay before Emil gripped the base of his shaft and lowered his head.

Emil started off slow, pressing his lips to Luke's hips, fingers lightly tracing the reddish ginger hair that travelled from his naval to the part Emil couldn't wait to have in his mouth. He kept kissing Luke's smooth skin and mouth-watering muscles and continued to tease Luke with his tongue, licking the head of his cock, then holding Luke's erection to run his tongue along the underside of its thick length. When Luke arched into his hand, Emil knew it was time to get a taste.

Opening his mouth wide, Emil wrapped his lips around the head of Luke's cock. Sucking hard, his cheeks hallowing, Emil groaned at the back of his throat, having fantasized about this for so long, the reality was even better than he imagined.

Hands snapped out to grasp his hair, Luke holding on as Emil swallowed down Luke's hot shaft, little by little, easing him into it before Luke tugged on his hair and Emil swallowed as much of Luke's cock as he could.\

Emil devoured him, tasting the saltiness of Luke's sweat, feeling his cock pulse in his mouth, and the sounds he had Luke making made Emil feel very pleased with himself. Moving his hand from Luke's thigh, Emil cupped Luke's balls, massaging them as he moved his head up and down, up and down until Luke uttered his name.

With one final suck, Emil released Luke with a pop, peering up out of hooded lashes, his own dick painfully erect. "Was it worth the wait?"

Luke barked out a laugh. "Now I know what I've been missing out on."

"We are just getting started, babe."

Emil got to his feet, stripping off his own pants and freeing himself, taking his cock in his hands and pumping it once, twice, before Luke pushed off the wall and put his hand over Emil's.

"Let me."

Luke's tone, all husky and filled with lust, as he stepped to the side, his cock brushing against Emil's thigh as he took over from Emil, gripping him tight and stroking, kissing the side of his neck, his jaw before Emil turned his head and they kissed slowly, licking and tasting as Luke's warm palm gliding over his fullness, a moan of pleasure escaping Emil's lips.

The sound of that pleasure seemed to make Luke feel brave, encouraged, jerking his hips forward so that they were skin to skin, his stroking picking up pace and testing Emil's own control. Emil reached around to stroke Luke and they both groaned.

Their kissing intensified and hands began to wander, until their bodies were flush against one another, hips surging forward so that skin slapped off the skin. Emil stroked down Luke's back, cupping his buttocks and Luke broke the kiss.

Emil squeezed the flesh and then pressed a kiss to Luke's jaw. "I also considered myself a man who loved to give a blowjob, that I was a dick man but I think with you, delicious as your cock was, I do like my hands on your ass."

Luke's cheeks reddened, his mind going to where Emil had intended. His flesh quivered under his palms, with Emil giving his ass one last squeeze with a wink, kissing Luke quickly on the lips before he pulled Luke toward the bed.

Emil pushed him down, making Luke sit that fine ass down on the edge of the bed. Separating Luke's thighs, Emil tilted Luke's head up, holding his green-eyed gaze, running his hands over his ginger hair.

"So, do you prefer to top or bottom? I'm versatile so it's all what you'd like."

The rush of red to Luke's cheek as he ducked his head, had Emil wondering what he had said to make Luke get so shy all of a sudden. Emil leaned in to kiss Luke again, but Luke slipped off the bed and faced away from Emil, shielding his face from him.

"Hey, what happened? Where'd you go?"

Luke didn't answer, his shoulders slumped so Emil cautiously placed his hand on his spine, felt the tremor and then wrapped his arms around Luke from behind, pulling Luke's back to his chest, skimming his hands down Luke's chest.

"We can wait, there's no need to rush," Emil whispered into Luke's ear.

"It's not that." Luke ground out the tension in his shoulders.

Emil slid around to face Luke, taking his face in his hands, startled by the flash of embarrassment in Luke's eyes.

A thought flashed in Emil's mind, but Emil felt like he should dismiss it. Then he considered the fact that Luke wasn't out to the general public, that he had never been pictured with any male friends other than his heterosexual friends. While Emil had been snapped with men, no one suspected that the men were actual dates that were discreet.

No, that couldn't be the reason why Luke was suddenly gone cold on him.

"Luke," Emil broached softly, tracing his thumb over the curve of Luke's bottom lip. "Did you know what I meant, asking what you preferred sexually?"

"Of course I do. I'm not a fucking idiot."

Anger laced his tone and Emil cupped his face, even more, forcing his eyes to stay focused on Emil's. "No one said that you were an idiot, Luke. I just wanted to know what you liked. What turns you on...it's best to know before."

Luke's cheeks felt scalding hot under his palms as a muscle in his jaw ticked, and he swallowed hard before he spoke, in a tone that was barely a whisper. "I don't know."

Emil's heart clenched in his chest and he felt a surge of pity toward the gorgeous man in front of him but Emil would never let him see it. Luke needed to be seduced, to be teased into revealing his desires but he needed to be open and honest with Emil before he would ever dare try and go any further. Communication was key no matter the sexual partner.

"Luke, I need to know." Emil coaxed, caressing his face. "Have you slept with another man before? Are you a virgin?"

Luke shuddered, releasing a sigh and then he was nodding, confirming Emil's suspicions.

CHAPTER TWENTY-ONE

Luke

LUKE FELT heat all over his face, almost making him dizzy as he nodded his head, embarrassed that he was standing naked in front of this gorgeous man and admitting that he was inexperienced as all hell. He couldn't even bear to look at Emil for fear that all he would see is pity.

He was a virgin who had pushed down all of his sexual desires in order to focus on his driving, but Emil made it impossible for him to deny himself any longer.

"Luke," Emil started softly, a gentle but firm hand on his chin before Emil forced Luke to look at him. "This does not change the fact I want to be with you. It just means I have to change my approach."

Emil brushed his lips against Luke's, then reached down to take Luke's erection in his hands and stroke as he said softly. "Does it make you harder to think about you sliding your dick into my ass, or would it make you come harder if it was my cock sheathed inside you?"

The image of him bent over as Emil thrust in and out of him make his cock twitch in Emil's hands and that made Emil chuckle in a husky tone. "Well, that answers that question."

Emil kissed him, slowly, teasing, trying to get Luke back in the mood, continuing the lazy strokes, his hand moving up and down his cock until Luke gripped Emil's face and kissed him hard. Their tongues and teeth and lips all collided, Emil walking them back toward the side of the bed.

Breaking the kiss, Emil let go of Luke to pump his shaft, then reached inside his bedside table and withdrew a box of condoms and a bottle of lube that made Luke blush furiously.

Luke watched fascinated as Emil popped open the lid of the lube and coated his fingers in it, a hungry expression on his face. Swallowing hard, his heart hammering inside his chest, Luke let himself be led in front of the mirror, Emil asking him to brace his hands on the wall, and spread his legs a little.

Emil arched Luke so that his ass was bared for Emil, the other man kissing Luke's spine, his tongue flickering out to lick down as far as the crack of his ass as Luke sucked in a breath.

"Emil..." Luke groaned, the sight of watching his cock twitch with every touch, every caress, Emil's dark eyes dancing mischievously in the mirror as Luke held his gaze and Emil trailed a finger down his spine, his other hand massaging his ass.

"I need to make sure that when I fuck you, you're ready to take my cock. Have you ever been fingered before?"

Luke shook his head, a mixture of lust and shame at Emil's blunt words, but then Emil smiled as if he liked the idea that the only man Luke had ever been with was Emil. Luke felt a slight intrusion as Emil slide a finger into his ass and mimicked sex, the feeling of strangeness lasting only a moment before Luke hissed through his teeth.

While Emil was stroking his finger in and out of Luke, the pressure in his cock was building and Luke wanted to reach down and grip it, yet, he didn't want to remove his hands from the wall, lest he disturb the feel of Emil's finger inside him.

But Luke needed more, wanted more.

"More." He managed to ground out, earning a dark laugh from Emil as he added a second finger and Luke found that he was arching his ass so Luke could get deeper.

"I think you're going to like the feel of my cock inside you, Luke."

Luke heard the moan tumbling from his lips and his entire body trembled at the thought of it, fire in his belly, shooting all the way down to his cock. "Emil, now."

Emil slowly withdrew his fingers, leaving Luke standing spread out, glancing over his shoulder as he saw Emil wipe his hands, then stand his cock up, unwrapping a condom and rolling it on. Luke clenched his ass, adrenaline spiking in his veins as Emil beckoned him over to the bed, as Emil applied more lube onto his condom, Luke's legs feeling wobbly as he did, letting Emil lay him down on the bed with another blistering kiss.

Luke was still facing the mirror, this time, he was braced half on his stomach, half on his side, his ass angled toward Emil as he climbed onto the bed beside him. Emil kissed the side of his neck, then murmured in his ear. "If I hurt you at all, tell me to stop."

Panic flared in Luke's chest at the feel of the head of Emil's cock at his entrance, his hand fisting the sheet. Emil slowly pushed into him, this penetration more invasive, more ...claiming than Emil's fingers had been. Luke felt himself being stretched as Emil withdrew then slowly slid back in, only to repeat and repeat until Luke forgot about his panic and his worry and let himself be engulfed in the pleasure.

The next time he felt Emil push into him, Luke pushed his ass back so that Emil was fully sheathed inside him. The moan that was elicited from both of them joined into one long exhilarating sound. Emil began to move in earnest, and Luke felt Emil restrain himself from thrusting harder, faster, careful to make it a pleasurable experience for Luke.

"Fuck, Emil. Harder. Faster. Gods, just fuck me." Luke wasn't sure his words were even coherent or if Emil was hearing him, the sound of Emil's heavy breathing filling Luke's own ears.

The Luke's words seemed to snap the restraint in Emil, as Luke felt himself be pulled to his knees on the bed, as Emil withdrew from him, one arm going around Luke's waist to hold him up, then Emil was pounding into him, Luke meeting Emil's thrusting by arching his back. Emil reached around with his free hand, gripping Luke's hot, hard length and sliding his hand up and down Luke's shaft with every powerful thrust of his cock.

The sound of their pants, their groans, the smell of sex and sweat, of Emil, the tight grip on his cock, and the utter sensations of being completely owned sent Luke over the edge, his bark of pleasure as he came in Emil's hand, his body shifting forward so his face was fully on the mattress.

Emil kept pumping Luke's cock, then he let go to grip Luke's hips, filling him once, twice more before Emil let out a long, sexy as sin groan before Luke felt him shudder inside him, his lover coming just a few moments after Luke had.

Emil collapsed on top of him, keeping their bodies locked together for a few more seconds before he disengaged, the feel of Emil's cock withdrawing dragging a gasp from Luke that had Emil grinning. Luke rolled over in the bed, the reminder that he had just had sex for the first time as he felt a little discomfort. He watched as Emil removed the condom, discarded it, then removed the duvet from the bed where Luke had orgasmed, throwing it in the washing basket.

Emil strode back to the bed, blanket in hand, then snuggled up next to him pulling the blanket over their waists. Luke lay on his back, trying to process what had just happened, as Emil shifted so that he lay on his side, looking down at Luke.

"Are you okay?" Emil asked as Luke reached up and caressed Emil's face.

"That was...amazing." Amazing seemed like a piss poor word for what had just happened between them but Luke felt like he was whole, for the first time in his life.

Emil bent his head and kissed Luke softly on the mouth. "Thank you for trusting me to be your first."

They kissed a little more, hands roaming freely now that the awkwardness of their first time was gone and Luke tasted every inch of Emil's skin, learning what he liked, what made Emil's breath hitch, what drove him to insanity and in turn, Luke learned the answers to all the questions that he had before regarding what it was that turned him on.

They kissed and showered then slept for the remainder of the night, waking in each other's arms. It was so easy to be with Emil, to pretend for even a moment that this was his life and would continue to be his life long after they left the rehabilitation centre.

The following morning, it was Emil who rolled on top of him, bringing their bodies flush together, his lips and hands working Luke into a frenzy, until all he could think about, all he could smell and feel was Emil, until Emil did something very wicked with his tongue and Luke lost himself in Emil.

He was starting to think that the answer to his question about what turned him on was Emil Anderson and Emil Anderson alone.

Chapter Twenty-Two

Luke

BEING with Emil made Luke deliriously happy and he felt like with Emil beside him, he could take on the world. It was so simple, in their little bubble. And by God, Emil was a voracious lover. It didn't take long for a kiss to turn into naked shower sex, or Luke getting bent over the couch and completely taken. He had always been a little embarrassed that he waited so long to lose his virginity but Emil had been worth the wait.

When they were together, whether it was eating a meal, having a kick about in the garden or curled up in bed watching a movie, Luke forgot about everything else going on in his life and lost himself in Emil. With the possibility of Emil being discharged soon, Luke had to admit he didn't know how to broach the subject of what happened next with them.

Because there was a very high chance Luke was in love.

The weeks had flown by and now, there were only two races left on the calendar and Noah was on the cusp of winning his first world championship. Today Luke had gotten special permission to leave the rehab facility to attend a dinner at Charlie's house. Emil looked striking in a pair of faded denim jeans, a t-shirt, and a Danish team bomber jacket.

Luke himself felt somewhat normal. Dressed in black jeans and a long-sleeved tee and he was bringing a hoody with him. Emil was reclining in his chair when Luke walked in, slowly getting to his feet and greeting Luke with a kiss that had him contemplating calling and saying that they would be late.

To be honest, Luke was feeling a little apprehensive. This was the first big event since he had woken up, and it was the first time he would be around everyone who had watched him almost die. It was also the first time he would be seeing Noah in the flesh since before the crash.

And Luke wasn't sure how he was to act with Emil. Quinn and Oskar knew that they were kind of a thing but since neither of them were out out, how was he to act? Did they ignore each other or just act friendly? It was all giving him a headache.

Oskar had offered to collect them, and Luke sat in the back of the car and listened to the easy banter of the two friends as they chatted away, with Emil trying his best to keep Luke involved in the conversation. It was a quick drive to Charlie's house, her childhood home, and a short walk toward the race track where Luke had first gotten into a formula one car.

When Oskar parked and they got out, Luke gazed over toward the race track and he sucked in a breath. Emil and Oskar had already headed toward the house when Emil realized that Luke wasn't with them.

"Are you okay?" Emil asked, brushing his fingers against Luke's.

"Yeah, I'm okay. Gimmie a minute and I'll be right in."

"Would you like some company"

Luke smiled, shaking his head. "I think this is something I need to do by myself."

Emil nodded letting his fingers linger before he strode back to the house and Luke walked down the path that led from Charlie's house to the race track. At night, the track was unusually quiet, with a few spotlights guiding the path to the road. The familiarity of it sang in Luke's bones and even he had to admit that the fact that he was able to stand here was a miracle in itself.

Luke crouched down and placed his palm on the tarmac and closed his eyes. This felt like coming home, and it was agony, and torment, and ecstasy all at once.

"I do the exact same thing every timc I've been away for what feels like too long."

Luke snorted at the sound of Noah's voice, rising

as he opened his eyes. "I remember. I remember the night that a new security guard called the guards because some unsavoury type was lying on the track and refused to move. Quinn got that habit from you."

Noah Donovan had eyes like cloudy skies and a handsome brooding face to match but he was also one of the best people Luke knew. Most of the time, Noah's expression didn't betray his emotions, and yet, tonight, he was looking at Luke like he didn't believe he was standing there talking to him.

"I should have let you come see me sooner," Luke offered, rocking back and forth on his feet. "And to say thank you. I know you tried to get to me when I was in the car. I heard your voice before I blacked out."

Noah didn't say anything, just gripped his shoulder and squeezed. "I would have walked through flames to try and get you, Luke."

Luke cleared his throat and tried to elevate Noah's pain. "Just another reason to have all the women fawning over you. They do go crazy for superheroes."

Noah barked out a laugh and shook his head. "Man, I've missed you. Smartass."

They walked back to the house, with Luke casting a glance over his shoulder before Noah held open the door and ushered Luke inside. Luke swallowed hard as they walked into the kitchen and the conversation immediately halted, making Luke blush when everyone looked at him.

"Hey." It certainly wasn't Shakespeare but Luke felt like he had to say something.

Gathered in the kitchen, smattered around the room, were some of the best people from sports and music. Charlie handed him a beer and then Luke was lost in a flurry of greetings and hugs and he was overwhelmed by the love and support. He spared a glance at Emil, who was over by the patio doors with Declan Walsh, lead singer of Heartache Melody, and Andi Collins, PR superstar and Declan's girlfriend, and Oskar as they talked about sports.

Noah was helping Charlie in the kitchen while Quinn was talking to Luna, who lifted her gaze to his and Luke could see that she was guarded as if she didn't know which Luke had arrived tonight. He smiled at Luna, hoping to show that he was happy to see her.

Luna handed off her drink to Quinn and came forward, stopping in front of him with her hands on her hips. "I see you got over your pity party and up off your ass."

The room had stopped to watch the exchange but Luke had been bickering and trading insults with Luna for years so this was just their way of showing that they loved one another.

"I'm glad to see that your manners have improved while I was, on my ass, as you said. I was certain that your new manager might have tried to at least house train you."

Luna flicked her braid off her shoulder. "Andi knows that being this fucking amazing is worth what I lack in manners. When you are this awesome, some things just slip through the cracks."

"Humble too, I see."

Luna grinned and flung herself at Luke, wrapping her arms around her neck and Luke chuckled, patting her on the back. "Hey, I know you love making a scene but this is too much."

The room laughed with them as Luna let go of Luke and punched him in the shoulder. "It's good to see you on your feet, big brother."

"It's good to be on my feet, little sister."

They both grinned at the inside joke, with Luna being a few minutes older than Luke but Luke had a few inches of height on Luna.

"Well, now that everyone's here, let's eat," Charlie said, putting the final few dishes on the table.

Luke didn't know where to sit as all the couples began to take a seat so, in the end, he took the vacated seat next to Emil. Dinner passed by quickly and it felt like no time had passed since they had last had meals together, with a few added bodies to their family.

After dinner, Luke helped clear the table and load the dishwasher, despite Charlie's attempts to get him to sit down. The rest of the crew were sitting in the living room and Luke sauntered over to the armchair that Emil was sitting on and perched himself on the edge of the seat.

"When do you head back to Denmark, Emil? It's been nice having you around." Oskar asked, taking a sip from his beer.

"Soon," Emil confirmed and Luke's heart sank, emotions swirling in him. "But I have some things that I need to do before I go back. And I have developed a taste for your Irish beer. I need more of that before I go."

Everyone laughed as Emil drained his beer and then his hand came down to rest on Luke's knee. Luke freaked out as everyone looked at them, causing Luke to bolt upright, a sting in his hip as he retreated to the kitchen to get Emil another drink.

Chapter Twenty-Three

Emil

MIL FELT heat in his cheeks as Luke dashed off and left him under the scrutiny of everyone's gaze. Oskar and Quinn shared a look and then Quinn went after Luke. Noah, thank the gods, started up a conversation and pulled Emil into it but if Emil was being honest, he was rather mad.

He supposed he should have asked Luke if they were going public, as they say, but it had felt like the most natural thing in the world to put his hand on Luke after all that they have shared. Luke had come back into the sitting area, handed Emil his beer, and then went to the farthest part of the room as far away from Emil as it seemed he could manage.

It had brought a bad atmosphere to what had been a splendid evening, and soon after, Oskar offered to drop them back to the facility. Everyone made warm, quick goodbyes and it was actually Luna who walked him out.

"I feel like I need to defend my brother from being such a dumbass."

Emil patted her arm. "There really is no need. Actions, they speak louder than words."

Luna glanced over her shoulder, then back at Emil. "Luke has always felt like people would judge him for his sexuality. That the world of motorsport would not accept him and that he would end up being known as the gay racer instead of a racer, has tripped him up. He didn't want the gender he was attracted to, to define him. Luke can break through hang-ups with you. Please don't give up on him."

Emil considered Luna's thoughts the entire journey back to the facility and when Luke got out and thanked Oskar before leaving the two friends alone, Emil could feel the anger building inside him.

"Don't," Oskar said, turning off the engine.

"Don't what?" Emil asked though he knew full well that Oskar would know that he was mad.

"You are not a man who is quick to anger, but even I can see that you are seething. Things can be said in the heat of the moment and I would not want you to say something you may regret tomorrow. I want you to be happy, Emil."

Oskar's wise words deflated some of his anger but not all of it.

"Does Luke know yet?" Oskar asked and Emil sighed.

"Not yet. I panned on telling him tomorrow."

"Do it now, Emil. Your decision may make it easier to know if you and Luke can have a future."

Emil waved Oskar off and then headed inside, taking a few deep breaths to try and calm himself further. Oskar was right, he needed to be upfront about everything and see if this was the turning point in their relationship.

Luke was waiting for him in Emil's room, a shadow of fear in his eyes and Emil knew that Luke understood that he had hurt Emil, and that his actions to Emil felt like a rejection. When Luke neglected to offer any kind of reason or apology, Emil felt his anger surge once again.

Folding his arms across his chest, Emil leaned in the doorway. "Would you like to explain to me why you did what you did?"

"I'm not sure. We hadn't talked about what this was."

"What this was? What this was? You mean whether it was just sex or whether or not you considered us to be in a relationship?" Emil ground out, almost snarling at Luke.

"It's more than just sex, Emil. I shouldn't have

reacted as I did. It was reflex. I didn't want to hurt you."

Luke sounded sorry, sounded like he meant the words he was saying. And Emil wanted to believe him, because even though they had not been too vocal about their feelings, Emil had fallen in love with Luke. But was this love enough to survive outside if the comfort of their privacy here?

"I need to know something," Emil said, as Luke got to his feet as if to come toward him, but Emil held up his hand to stop Luke. "Do you see us as having a future? Do you see us sitting in a restaurant and you holding my hand without checking to see if anyone is looking? Can you kiss me in front of our friends and family and be proud to stand with me?"

"I – I ..." Luke stammered, giving Emil the answer that he hadn't wanted to hear and his heart sank.

"Because I would have been proud to have you walk a red carpet with me. I would have held your hand in a restaurant and looked into your eyes and not cared who was looking at us. I would have been delighted to have you touch me in front of all our friends and I would have not fled as if your touch disgusted me."

Luke ran his hands through his hair. "That's not what I meant. I'm sorry. I'm just not as comfortable with PDA. I don't know if I ever will be."

"That wasn't PDA, Luke. It was my hand on your knee. It was the same as Declan having his hand on the small of Andi's back. It was the same as Oskar tucking a strand of Quinn's hair behind her ear, or Noah taking Charlie's hand and holding on until she walked far away and their fingertips were the last things to touch."

Emil stared deep into Luke's green eyes as he said. "If you cannot bear to touch me when surrounded by all the people who actually know that you are gay, then how can you do anything like I said? I want to be with you, but I won't do that in the shadows. I cannot."

"Wait, Emil, listen." Luke pleaded with him. "I made a mistake. But I'm not out. I don't know when I will be. Can't we just continue as we are? We can figure out the rest later."

Emil wanted to concede to Luke, because the thought of not being with him didn't sit well with Emil but he had already pulled the trigger on his own pursuit of living in his truth and he was starting to believe that perhaps, Luke was not to be a part of it.

"I'm afraid that I can no longer continue as we are. I have decided I can no longer hide from who I am." Despite the cracking of his heart, Emil felt the rightness in his words, in the decisions he had committed to. "All of my meetings in the last two weeks were preparing so that I could be honest with myself. I told my family who I was. I told my manager and my team. I plan on telling the world who I really am. I've already had an interview about it."

"You didn't tell them about me, did you?"

Luke's face had paled with every word Emil had spoken and with one sentence, Emil knew that he and Luke could have no future at all. And it devasted him.

"And there is my answer. You should be congratulating me for being brave and being myself. You should be asking me if I am okay and if my family were okay with who I was. You should be commending me for all of that and all you are worried about is if I outed you? Do you think that little of me?"

In Luke's defence, he looked crestfallen, but Emil could not afford to be held back by Luke, who had to make his own mind up about stepping out of the shadows and into his life.

Emil went to the wardrobe and took out his duffel bag and then Luke sprang into motion.

"Wait, Emil. Don't go. We can talk about this. Sleep on it, and then we can talk."

Emil laughed darkly, shaking his head. "I was cleared to leave weeks ago. But I stayed...for you. I sacrificed returning to the sport I love to help you get back to the sport you love. When you were drowning, I stayed to help you stay afloat. I did all of that because I was in love with you."

"I love you too, Emil. Please don't leave me. We can work it out."

Emil wanted nothing more than to believe that working it out was possible. That Luke would be proud to walk down the streets he called home, hand in hand with him. He didn't think that this would ever be the case.

"Then call Charlie and tell her that you want to come forward about our relationship."

Luke had been moving towards him but ground to a halt at his words. "I...I ...Emil, please. I can't."

"Then we have nothing more to say. Goodbye Luke."

Emil left the room to the sound of Luke crying, his heart shattering but it felt in his bones that he needed to walk away, even if walking away from Luke was the hardest thing he had to do. Even if it felt like he was leaving a little piece of his heart behind him.

CHAPTER TWENTY-FOUR

Luke

LUKE HAD SEEN the effect of heartbreak on others before, had seen his sister after countless boyfriends couldn't deal with her take no prisoners attitude. He had witnessed Noah and how his love and separation from Charlie had impacted him. He had seen just how broken Jameson was for years after losing Layla.

But Luke was naïve. He hadn't understood just how bereft heartbreak could leave you. He had never been in love before and that emotion, it was stronger than the sum of all his fears and Luke could never have expected to feel such ... such... loss, the moment Emil had walked away from him.

Multiple calls to Emil had gone unanswered. Luke

didn't even know if he was still in the country until the Danish soccer team had posted an update on their socials, with a picture of Emil and Oskar at a restaurant in a very well-known hotel in Cork that had the caption: "Ireland has been good to our new captain. But we are delighted that Emil is on his way back to us. See you soon." #proudofourcaptain

And the pride that Luke should have had when Emil told him that he was coming out sparked in his chest. Becoming captain of your national team was one of the greatest honours any sportsperson could have, and Emil had earned his captaincy.

The article that Emil had told Luke about was published yesterday and the support in the sports community had been fantastic. The world loved Emil and they had blown up Emil's social media in the comments with overwhelming acceptance.

Luke had read and reread the article over and over and over, with one line in the article bringing tears to his eyes because even before their argument, before their split, Emil had told the interviewer his life story without mentioning his name. When asked why Emil thought it was so hard for sportsmen and women to be open about their sexuality, Emil had responded,

"People are easy to slip to judgement. You hear it in the media every day, the first man of colour, the first Asian woman, the first woman to do something etc. I think most athletes, no matter the discipline, they don't want their race, their gender, or their sexuality to be the first topic of conversation. Who I am as an athlete is not defined by my sexuality. I am Emil Anderson, Danish footballer. When I am on the pitch, that is all that should matter."

And with the outpouring of support Emil had received, it was all that mattered.

Luke wanted to be brave like Emil. He wanted to have the courage to be less afraid.

Mark had distracted Luke by telling him that they had a few more tests to run and then he would be discharged to continue his rehab as an outpatient. The last couple of days had been a barrage of tests, both medical and physical and Luke was ready to get back to normal.

Even if that was without Emil.

Today, he felt like he was waiting to go to the principal's office because there was to be a medical review and Luke was hoping that he would get the all-clear to start preparing to get back in the car. If he had to lose Emil, then he just had to make it back to the sport he loved and since he was feeling so fit, Luke knew it was only a matter of time.

Quinn had told him earlier this week that Charlie was looking at reserve drivers for next season, since Quinn would be starting off her season in the car, and maybe, when he got the all-clear today and if he trained even harder, then Charlie might agree to having him as reserve driver.

Mark came and got him late in the afternoon, far

later than Luke had expected and he certainly wasn't expecting to see so many people gathered. A large TV was set up to the side with Charlie on the screen on zoom, , from the looks of it in her mobile office from halfway across the world she had her boss mode face on but did wave at Luke when he entered.

One or two more doctors came in as Luke lowered himself into a chair at the end of the room. Sweat ran down his spine and he wiped his palms down his joggers. His main doctor, the one who had diagnosed the inflammation lifted her head and gave Luke a smile.

"Luke, sorry for the delay."

"It's all good. Hit me with it, doc."

Luke should have known when the smile dropped that something wasn't right, but Luke had truly believed that his luck had to change. And yet, it was about to get worse.

"We are ready to discharge you in a few days but we have to be realistic about the path before you. We have extensively examined and re-examined all your scans, and while your recovery has been amazing, we cannot sign off on you returning to driving an F1 car. I am sorry, Luke."

"Wait," Luke croaked out, aware that his vision had blurred as he tried to stop himself from crying. "I've got no pain. I can walk again. I've been in a car and I feel fitter than I did before the crash. Why are you counting me out now? Why not give it more time?"

The doctor took off her glasses and set them down on the table. "Time will not fix the issue in your hip. You know more about F1 than any of us in this room but the science doesn't lie. The inflammation in your hip can and will return. The broken bone you suffered in your pelvis and hip, right where the joint is, is fragile. Getting into a car that has downforce and gravitational force or as you say G force, could be life-limiting in another crash. You can go on to drive again, just not in formula one."

Nausea rolled in Luke's stomach. this couldn't be it – this couldn't be how it ended.

"And what about in a year or two?" He asked, already knowing the answer.

"This is something that would more likely get worse, not better. Surgery may be needed in the future to keep it stable." The doctor glanced at Charlie before she looked back at Luke and continued. "I know this is not what you wanted to hear, Luke, and we will continue to monitor your progression but we had to be honest on your outlook since we plan on discharging you."

"I want a second opinion." He ground out as he waited for the doctor to speak but it was Charlie's voice that came next.

"Luke, that was the first thing I did when they told me. I got a second and a third opinion. They all said the same. If you were to crash again in an F1 car, then loss of life would be probable. We can't risk losing you again. I'm sorry."

What the fuck was the point in all this rehab if not to get back in the car? What was the point in him working his ass off for nothing? What was the point in him pushing Emil away if the career he had worked so hard for was now gone? What was the point in him being alive, if everything that made him feel like his heart was worth beating had been taken away from him?

"Who am I without the car, Charlie? What's the point of me if I'm not Luke Sullivan, Rebel Racers driver? How do I live with the fact that the dream I've had since I was a boy has been taken away from me and it wasn't even my fault?" Luke surged to his feet and guffawed. "You can't risk me but who I was died the moment my career was ended in that crash. I fought and fought and what did it get me? Sweet fuck all. I'd have been better off if I died in the crash than be forced to live this purgatory."

Luke was already walking out of the room to the sound of Charlie's gasp of horror but Luke didn't care. He was done. It was over and there was no point in lingering about and hearing all the apologies and all the pitying expressions. All the hope that he had kept inside him had evaporated and now he stood, twenty-four years old with no future, no career and he had also lost the man he loved because he had chosen a dead career over the chance of happiness.

It was over for him now and Luke knew that in his bones. He numbly placed one foot in front of the other, ignoring the buzz of his phone as Luke ignored the receptionist, ignored everything around him, and strode right out the main door of the rehab facility to find the nearest place that would sell him alcohol so Luke could drink himself to oblivion.

Chapter Twenty-Five

Emil

If Emil needed any validation that he had made the right decision, the outpouring of love from across the globe would have definitely given him that. His family had been amazing, with his sisters scolding him for not telling them sooner, but he assured Lærke and Karla that he had meant to tell them, however, he hadn't been aware that he was hiding it. His mother had been wonderful too and he was looking forward to heading home tomorrow night

Emil had seen the mountain of texts from Luke, yet couldn't bring himself to open any of them. He missed Luke. He really did. He missed the little routine they had gotten into. Emil had gotten used to falling asleep curled up against Luke's body and walking up in a tangle of limbs.

It had taken every bit of Emil's discipline and self-control not to pick up the phone and call him, or to drive out to the rehab facility and try and see if the prospect of Emil walking away for good had changed Luke's perspective even a little bit.

Oskar had been his usual supportive self and Emil loved him for it. After the article was published, Oskar had stayed in Ireland rather than fly out with the team for the penultimate race. They had gone down to the hotel for dinner, and Emil had signed a few autographs and smiled for pictures until they had been ushered into a private area for their food.

When Emil had been uncharacteristically quiet, Oskar had tried to fill up the silence.

"You miss him?"

Emil pushed his food around his plate before lifting his gaze to Oskar. "Am I that easy to read?"

"No usually. Then again, you are usually more vocal about things than I am."

That had Emil chuckling, his friends sometimes icy exterior shielding the kind heart and soul in Oskar. He was lucky, all those years ago, to have found Oskar, or for him to find Emil.

"Are you calling me a loudmouth?" Emil asked with a smile.

"Perhaps."

Emil let loose a chortle of laughter that had some diners looking in their direction. Oskar took a sip from his pint and then said softly. "Quinn said Luke misses you too."

"Are you trying to play matchmaker, Oskar?"

Oskar snorted, rolling his eyes. "Far from it. I am merely stating a fact. If you two are as miserable as one another, then can you not try and work it out so that you are less miserable?"

Emil dropped his fork and leaned back in his seat, running a hand through his hair. "It is not as simple as that."

"It could be." Oskar replied, resting his elbows on the table and leaning in closer. "That was what you said to me all those months ago when I was all twisted up inside about my feelings for Quinn. It could be. Quinn thinks Luke pushed you away because he is scared that if he comes out, and the press is negative, his career might never recover."

Huffing out a breath, Emil drawled. "Then we are on two different journeys and the paths don't line up. I want what you have with Quinn. A partner. Someone to build a life with. Someone who isn't ashamed to hold my hand in public or private. Someone to dance with at events so I do not have to go alone. I would like to spend boring nights in front of the tv."

Oskar's lips curved into a smile. "For someone who used to spend his youth telling me of all the glitz and glam that he was going to indulge in when he was a famous footballer, that life sounds very tame."

While Oskar was right that Emil had once loved all

the notoriety that came with being a footballer, over the years, it had frayed on his nerves and gotten old quite quickly. And now, now that he knew exactly what he wanted in life, the person he pictured doing all those mundane things with couldn't be there for him like that.

"You used to spend your days searching for adrenaline and now you are content with a slower pace."

"If you think having a girlfriend who drives a race car is a slower pace, then you do not know what life with Quinn is like. But yes, I get to travel the world with the woman I love and there is nothing more that I enjoy doing but spending time with her alone – "

"I bet." Emil quirked his brow and Oskar laughed.

"Get your mind out of the gutter. If you had let me finish, I would have said that spending an evening curled up on the couch watching some silly rom-com that Quinn says she hates but secretly loves, is one of my favourite things. But I will deny it if you ever tell her."

Oskar's face lit up when he spoke of Quinn, and Emil was jealous of his friend but he did not begrudge him. Emil could never begrudge Oskar his happiness when his life had been filled with sickness and sadness.

"If it's hurting you this much, Emil, then perhaps it is worth a second chance. But whatever you decide, know that I am always here for you."

They had finished up not long after that and Oskar had hugged him, telling him that he would see him in a week or so for the end of years Rebel Racers charity dinner. Emil had been uncertain of whether or not to make the trip back, considering most of the Rebel Racers team were Luke's friends and Emil wasn't sure, after what happened the night in Charlie's, that he would be welcome again.

But Quinn had assured him that once he was considered part of the family, they didn't tend to let people go, even if they were being stubborn idiotic donkeys.

Emil hadn't been sure if Quinn was referring to Luke or him, or perhaps both.

Tonight, Emil had this feeling of dread in his stomach that made him so restless he had gone down to the hotel gym to work off his frustration, but it hadn't done much. He'd showered and ordered room service but his appetite wasn't really there. He contemplated going to bed to try and get some sleep before his car arrived to take him to Dublin airport, and yet he knew that there was no chance that actually happening, especially when all he could think about was the fact Luke wasn't laying beside him.

Emil picked up his phone and scrolled through it, realizing that he didn't even have a photo of himself and Luke together and Emil didn't know if that was a blessing or a curse. Opening up one of his social media apps, Emil went right to Luke's page and the last picture was one before his accident, with Luke and Quinn posing after a day karting and Luke looked so happy.

Sitting down on the edge of the bed, Emil began to

analyse Luke's expression and his pictures, and anywhere he looked happy or content, Emil wondered if Luke had looked as happy as he did in the photos when he was with him. How much of those cheeky, beaming photos of Luke were of him actually being happy, and how much was fake?

Emil must have fallen down the rabbit hole of scrolling through Luke's pictures when his phone vibrated in his hand and out of shock and surprise, Emil dropped the phone and it slid under the bed. Cursing, he scrambled to the floor and reached under the bed to grab the phone, frowning when he saw two missed calls from Oskar, and just as he went to call him back, Oskar rang again and now Emil was worried.

"Oskar, apologies I dropped my phone?"

"Have you seen Luke?" Oskar's voice came down the line, insistent.

"No, I assume he's back at the rehab. What's going on?"

Oskar swore before there was a jostling and Quinn came on the line. "Hey Emil, has Luke tried to contact you today?"

Emil told Quinn that he hadn't heard from Luke and then asked her what was going on. But it was Oskar that spoke next, "I've put you on speaker. Luke had an appointment this afternoon with the doctors and they told him that he would never drive in a formula one car again. Charlie said he was upset and then he walked from the room. They thought he'd gone to cool off but it seems he walked right out the door and nobody's seen or heard from him since. We are all overseas so we can't do anything."

Emil's heart broke for Luke and Emil knew that if he was told he could never play football again that he would be devastated. Worry filled his veins at the thought of Luke out there, by himself, grieving for the loss of his childhood dream.

"Emil?" Quinn said, her voice cracking. "I know you two are not on the best of terms right now. And I hate to ask but can you call him? Can you help me find my brother?"

CHAPTER TWENTY-SIX

Luke

LUKE WAS on his second bottle of vodka as he ambled down the street, staggering and having to lean against the wall to stop himself from listing over. He had called Rhys, Andi's brother, to see if there was a party Luke could lose himself in but Rhys hadn't bothered to answer him. They weren't really friends, but Rhys had always been a reliable source when it came to getting wasted.

He'd already gotten thrown out of one pub for starting a fight, and another wouldn't have a bar of him, denying him entry. He'd gone into a shop then and bought two bottles of cheap vodka, one he'd drank while sitting outside the post office on Oliver Plunkett

Street before the guards had moved him along and tried to confiscate his second bottle until the younger of the two recognised Luke and told him to go home and sleep it off.

Instead, Luke stumbled his way to the swanky hotel Emil was staying in and staggered inside, much to the horror of the receptionist behind the desk.

"What room is Emil Anderson in?" Luke slurred his words as the receptionist shook her head.

"I'm sorry, sir. We cannot give out guest information like that."

"Emil!" Luke shouted, the sound of Emil's name reverberating around the empty hotel lobby. "Emil!"

"Sir, if you don't leave, I'll have no choice but to call the guards."

Luke laughed, taking a drink from his vodka. "Call him. tell him I want to see him. He'll see me if you tell him."

The receptionist must have alerted someone in security because an aging security guard came from around the corner and headed toward Luke. Ambling around the security guard, Luke walked towards the elevator but the security guard moved forward and grabbed Luke by the arm.

"All right, lad. That's enough of that. Out ya go."

The bottle of vodka slipped from his fingers and smashed all over the lobby floor. Luke swore and shoved away from the security guard. "Look whatcha done. I just want to see him! Please let me see him?"

The security guard grabbed for him again, but Luke dodged, losing his balance and hitting the wall as the doors to the elevator opened and Emil stepped out, his eyes widening when he saw Luke.

From the very first moment Emil had stepped into his life, Luke had been transfixed by just how breathtaking he was. Even now, dressed in loose tracksuit bottoms and a long-sleeve tee, his hair disheveled and those dark eyes on him, Luke *craved* his touch.

"Hey baby." Luke ground out, ignoring the security guard who glanced from Luke to Emil.

"Sir, do you know this man?"

Luke was still slumped against the wall as Emil beckoned the security guard over whilst typing on his phone. The man then looked over his shoulder at Luke as Luke tried to make himself stand up straighter. The security guard and Emil shared a few more words and then Emil came forward and wrapped an arm around Luke's waist.

"Let's get you upstairs."

Luke leaned into the curve of Emil's neck and inhaled the scent of him. "You smell good."

"And you smell like you bathed in alcohol." Emil's tone was clipped and angry, not that Luke blamed him.

The moment they were in the elevator, Luke twisted so that he was facing Emil, putting his palms on Emil's chest. "I've missed you."

"Luke, you need to sleep it off."

"I think I'd prefer to get you off." Luke flashed Emil a drunken grin, the other man not looking as horrified as Luke imagined he would be by his unfiltered words and Luke could see the flicker of lust in Emil's eyes.

"Stop, Luke. We're done."

Luke pushed away and cradled his head in his hands. "I know. I know I fucked up and I know I've lost you but I feel like I'm adrift and I can't find my feet again but when I'm with you, I don't feel like that and I need to feel like I am someone, something."

He knew he probably wasn't making much sense as the elevator opened and Emil lead him to his room. Emil swiped his card and let them in. Luke's heart plummeted when he saw the packed suitcases.

"Luke, I'm sorry about-"

Luke didn't give Emil a chance to say anything, he pounced, crushing his lips to Emil's, moaning at the same time as Emil. Luke walked them back until Emil's back was against the wall and their bodies were flush against one another's.

Dragging his lips from Emil's mouth, Luke tilted Emil's head to kiss his throat, and Luke felt a thrill coarse throw him when Emil shuddered. Luke sucked on his neck, licked up the column of Emil's throat and Emil's hands went to Luke's hips.

"Please, Emil. Please."

Luke wasn't really sure what he was begging Emil for; to stay, to love him, to let him know his body one last time even if it ruined him when Emil left. It might be the ruination of him, but still, Luke chased the rush, chased Emil, even if he crashed and burned once the man he loved left him all alone.

"Please, Emil. Please."

He repeated his words, dropping to his knees as his hands slid up Emil's thighs to his slender hips before his fingers fumbling at the drawstring on his pants as Emil caught his hands and said. "Wait."

Luke lifted his eyes, looking up at Emil under hooded lashes. Licking his lips, Luke and Emil's eyes clashed as Emil said. "I am still leaving tomorrow."

"I know," Luke replied. "Let me know you one last time. Let me love you one last time. Please say yes, Emil."

Torn. That was the only way to describe the look on Emil's face as Luke yanked out Emil's tee and splayed his hands on Emil's stomach, the muscles bunching under his touch. Luke leaned in when Emil pulled off his tee and pressed his lips to the golden skin.

"Luke."

His name sounded like a curse as if Emil was cursing him for doing this but Luke didn't care. Luke undid the string at Emil's waist and yanked down his joggers, delighted that Emil was commando underneath, freeing Emil's cock and Luke's mouth watered at the sight of the thick hard shaft and he just had to have a taste.

Luke wrapped his hand round the base of Emil's

cock and stroked it, the other man's hands slamming against the wall as Luke dipped his head and licked the underside of his pulsating cock.

"Fuuuuuccck." Emil ground out, his head snapping down to watch as Luke stroked Emil and Luke grinned up at him.

With his free hand, Luke gripped Emil's muscular thigh, with Emil held in place by the joggers around his ankles and Luke's firm grasp on his leg. Luke stroked down his cock and then slid his hand down to cup Emil's balls and the moan that came out of Emil made Luke's own cock twitch.

He massaged Emil's sac, then shifted his hand back up to grip the base of his shaft once again and stopped, just halted his seduction and looked up at Emil who was breathing heavily as he locked eyes with Luke.

"Please, Emil. *Please*."

Emil closed his eyes for a moment and when he opened them again, Luke knew the answer was going to be yes even before Emil groaned out. "I'm still leaving tomorrow."

"I know. I fucking know. Just tonight, Emil. Just one more night."

Luke slid his hand up, stroking once as he leaned down and flicked his tongue over the head of Emil's cock.

"Yes, Luke...dear god yes."

Luke closed his mouth around the head of Emil's thick member and sucked hard, pausing for a moment before he began to take more and more of Emil into his mouth. He licked and sucked as Emil began to thrust into his mouth, his hands going to Luke's hair, holding him exactly where he wanted him. Luke breathed in and out of his nose, taking Emil all the way to the back of his throat, Emil holding him there until he gagged and then Emil pulled his hips back.

His hands roamed up to cup Emil's firm ass, forcing Emil to arch into his suction, his cheeks hallowing as he felt Emil tense and then he barked out Luke's name, coming hard into his mouth and Luke swallowed it all down until Luke had wrung him dry and he finally released Emil's spent cock from his mouth.

The gravity of the ending threatened to undo Luke, and from the look in Emil's eyes, his lover was feeling the same way. But Luke wasn't ready for it to end, just yet, or ever as he got to his feet, pulled off his own t-shirt, and kicked off his shoes before taking Emil's hand and dragging him towards the bed.

"I'm not finished with you just yet."

CHAPTER TWENTY-SEVEN

Luke

EMIL HAD BEEN GONE the morning after and Luke had woken with a bitch of a hangover. But it was nothing compared to the emptiness in his chest when Luke had woken and seen that Emil had left, probably not long after they'd had sex, once in the bed with Luke sliding slowly in and out of Emil and then once in the shower with Emil pounding into him from behind.

Luke had let himself out of the hotel, sending a message to advise everyone that he was okay but needed a few days to himself to sort his head out. Then he had checked himself into another hotel and took the time to strategize and come to terms with the shitty outcome.

The days bled into one another, as Luke took the time to see what he could do now and what he wanted for his future. It hurt, trying to come to terms with the reality that he could never race in Formula 1 again. He didn't know if he could stand on the sidelines and watch his best friends in the sport he loved, never to feel that rush again.

He needed to figure out who he was without racing, and that was hard for Luke because he didn't know who he was if he wasn't a racer. What skills did he have that could translate into the real world? How could he adjust to working nine to five? Would he always be this person who was angry that his career was cut short and how long before the resentment made him bitter and he couldn't find joy in life?

And then there was Emil...

Luke missed him like crazy, and even the fact that they hadn't shared the words I love you, Luke did love him. He wanted to be the type of man that Emil deserved, one that felt comfortable in his own skin enough to take the hand of the man he loved and walk down the street without caring who saw them. He wanted to go to dinner with his friends and family and kiss and touch his lover without his fear overshadowing him.

He wanted to be brave. And he wanted to be with Emil.

It was only in the dead of night, after another sleepless night that Luke had an epiphany, when his mind's overthinking kept him awake did the questions come to him.

Did he think he could live without F1? Luke knew it would be hard but he could, if he truly wanted to get the most out of his second chance.

Did he think that he could live without Emil? From the way that his stomach went queasy and his heart ricocheted in his chest, Luke knew the answer was a resounding no.

It had spurred him into action, sending an email to Charlie asking for a meeting with her and Andi when they returned from the last race of the season. Charlie had emailed back immediately and told Luke to come around to the house the following Wednesday at midday.

Luke had called his sister then and told Luna that he would be staying in the hotel for another couple of days and would she come see him. When Luna came by, Luke told her of his plans and Luna had been so supportive, it had made his decision easier.

The weekend was a test for Luke as he tuned in to watch Noah and Quinn in the final race of the season. He wanted to see if he could stand it, the watching without the pressure of too many people around and it surprised him how much he enjoyed being a spectator again. Noah and one of the Red Bull drivers were nearly level on points but Noah would have to win the race tomorrow to be crowned champion because of the loss of points on the race weekend that Luke had crashed.

Quinn had a squirrelly moment in qualifying, almost hitting the wall and Luke had leaned forward in his seat until she reigned the car in but only finished fifth. Luke hadn't felt too bad after that but he had felt absolutely devasted the following day when Noah lost out on the world championship by one point.

When he turned off the TV, he texted Noah to say he was sorry that Luke had cost him the championship and after an hour or two, Noah had messaged back to say that he would rather end up second and have Luke around than to finish first and know that Luke wasn't there.

Wednesday came around quickly and Luke, having commandeered the keys to his Ferrari back from Luna, then drove over to Charlie's and Noah's, spotting Noah's Audi and a Mini Cooper that had to be Andi's. Luke switched off the engine and steeled himself against what he was planning on doing.

He was terrified.

Luke got out of the car and knocked on the door, waiting until Charlie let him in, then he stepped inside, letting her close the door before she held out her arms and he stepped into her embrace. Charlie patted his back, giving him a warm smile as she led him into the kitchen where Andi was making coffee.

"You want a cup?" Andi asked, and Luke nodded his head, glancing around the room.

"Where's Noah?" Luke asked Charlie.

"He went for a run," Charlie told him, taking a seat on the couch and Luke followed suit. "He wasn't sure if you wanted him here for the meeting, since you only asked for me and Andi. He'll be back soon."

Andi came over with their coffees and then took a seat across from Luke. He squirmed in his seat as the woman waited for him to start and now that he was here, Luke wasn't sure how to begin. It must have shown on his face because Charlie set her coffee down. "It's okay, Luke. Whatever it is, it's okay."

Somehow, Luke actually believed her.

"I'm tired," Luke said quietly, his knee bouncing with nerves. "I'm tired of only living a half live and being utterly terrified of letting people see me. I hid behind the fact that I wanted to be judged on my merit and now, now that's gone and I didn't know how tired I was."

Swallowing hard, Luke sighed before continuing. "I nearly died. And I was so focused on getting back in the car that I didn't quite comprehend just how lucky I was. Or how empty my life was. I didn't realize just how lonely I was."

"Oh, Luke." Charlie had tears in her eyes she reached over and took his hand, and his own tears blurred his vision.

"I thought I was nothing without racing. But

losing it has made me realize I was only existing and then...then I fell in love and I realized that I could survive without being an F1 driver but I can't keep going as I am. I understand if this isn't something either of you can help me with, now that I'm not a part of the team anymore, but I wanted family to advise me on what to do."

Charlie's face grew serious. "Listen here, Luke Sullivan. You might not be driving the car any more but you will always, ALWAYS, be part of the team. You will always be a part of this highly dysfunctional family. You hear me?"

Luke chuckled. "Yes, boss."

"The offer I made to you is still there, Luke. Take the time to think on it but I assume you asked for us here for another reason."

"I don't think I could do a press conference but I need to retire in public and I need to be honest about who I am. I need to stop living in fear and grab hold of life because I know that the things you love can be taken from you in the blink of an eye." Luke inhaled sharply. "I lost the man I love because I was too scared to be myself. I let him walk away because I didn't think I could be with him the way he wanted. But I don't want to hide anymore."

"I know a reporter who would love to be involved in this. She's very discreet and professional. If you're sure that's what you really want?"

"It is. If you both come with me."

Charlie squeezed his hand. "We would be honoured."

The front door opened and Luke could hear the distinctive trance music coming from Noah's head-phones as his friend strode into the room, took off his headphones, and grabbed a bottle of water from the fridge. Noah strode over and held out his fist for Luke to bump.

"What I miss?" Noah asked, taking in his fiancé's tear-stained cheeks and Andi's fierce expression then looked to Luke.

Luke blew out a breath. "The girls are gonna help me come out of the closet."

It felt right, it felt so damn right as his friend grinned. "About damn time, about damn time."

CHAPTER TWENTY-EIGHT

Emil

EMIL FIDGETED with the collar of his shirt, uncomfortable to be standing in a room full of Rebel Racers staff and sponsors. Everyone had been very welcoming when he walked in, linking arms with Quinn, and Oskar on her other side. The hotel they had booked for the event was rather glamourous and while Emil had been in lots of fancy hotels since becoming a footballer, he was starting to believe that the world of motorsport was way more extravagant than football.

The ballroom of the hotel was on the ground floor, with a sweeping staircase that brought you down to the dance floor. There was a red carpet trailing down the stairs and reporters and media on either side snapping photos. The gothic-style room, complete with candelabras, thick black curtains, and furniture that was so gold and bright that Emil was starting to wonder if it was real gold.

Waiters and waitresses sauntered about with flutes of champagne that had various fruits in them and food that was so small, Emil wondered if everyone was hungry. One of the waitresses came over to them as soon as they had descended the stairs, but Quinn waved her away, winking at Emil as she headed to the bar and came back with three bottles of beer.

"Oh, this one is definitely a keeper, Oskar."

Oskar's lips curved into a smug smile as he bent down to kiss Quinn's cheek. "I know."

The woman in question rolled her eyes, but from the glint in her eyes, it was obvious that Quinn felt the same about Oskar. They looked like a royal pair, both dressed in black suits, Oskar wearing a dark blue shirt that seemed to make his eyes look glacier in colour but Quinn wore a form-fitting suit, trainers, and a short black top that kissed her naval, a long blazer style jacket thrown on.

There was a rapturous roar of applause as Emil turned to see Noah Donovan and Charlotte Coyle coming in, with Declan Walsh and Andi Collins following them. Emil allowed himself a moment of pity for the man who had lost the world title on a one-point margin, but looking at how Noah's arm was around Charlie's waist, the man smiling, you would never know he was hiding any devastation.

Declan Walsh was donating a guitar signed by all the members of Heartache Melody for the children's auction, so it made sense that he be here in person. Emil himself had called Oskar and asked would they be interested in a signed jersey from him, and Oskar told him that they would be delighted.

The jersey in question was the one he had worn just last week when he had played a charity game of football and had worn the captain's armband for the first time. When he jogged out onto the field, his team had been standing to give him a guard of honour and handed him this special jersey, one that had the pride flag on it. His eyes had brimmed with tears as they also wore pride armbands.

It might have been a friendly charity game but it would be one of the most important games of his career, especially since he got to share it with his family and with Oskar, who had travelled with him to Denmark and even played a little in the match.

Emil had been a bit nervous about coming back to Ireland, however, Oskar had assured him that everyone wanted him to be there. Oskar was careful not to mention Luke, who had not even tried to contact him after their whirlwind night in the hotel, and Emil wasn't sure if that was a blessing or if the well of bitter disappointment meant that he would never shake this morose feeling.

This morning Rebel Racers had released a statement to say that Luke had made a fantastic recovery from his injuries but after extensive consultation with doctors, both Rebel Racers and Luke himself decided that, for medical reasons, and with great disappointment, Luke would retire from racing. They made it clear that Luke would always be part of the Rebel Racers family.

Emil had wanted to reach out and make sure that Luke was okay, however opening that door may not be the healthiest for him. Luke was on a different path than he was and maybe in time, they could be in a room like this and be able to have a conversation without it being painful.

In the car on the way here, Quinn had been reluctant to give Emil an answer about if Luke was attending tonight. Emil had decided that he would stay until the auction of the jersey and then slip out before anyone realized he was gone, to minimize any risk of running into Luke.

Someone tapped on the microphone and everyone hushed as they announced the auction would start in about ten minutes. Quinn pulled Oskar off to go and speak to Charlie, leaving Emil standing by himself at the table. But he wasn't alone for long.

"You look like you'd rather be anywhere but here."

Emil snorted and glanced up at Noah, the handsome racer with rain clouds in his eyes. "I find I would be more at home covered in mud and grass than dressed in fancy clothes."

"Ya, not too fond of the penguin suit myself but Charlie said I'd never get away with wearing jeans. I didn't argue. I know when to retreat from battles I can't win."

Laughing at the racer, Emil asked the waitress for two beers and handed one to Noah, who nodded at him. They stood silent for a moment, the awkwardness making Emil squirm a little.

"Listen, I know that you and me barely know each other so feel free to tell me to fuck right off, but Luke's my brother. I didn't know what it was like to have a family until I joined Rebel Racers or what having siblings was like, but Luke made me family from day one. He didn't hide who he was from me. Or Quinn. He is one of the kindest, most loyal people I know and he is worth taking a chance on."

Setting his beer down on the table in front of him, Emil sighed. "I know all of that. But we want different things and I would not want to grow to resent him. Or have him resent me."

Noah opened his mouth to respond when they announced the auction was about to start. It passed by quite quickly, with many items selling for ridiculous amounts of money. The Heartache Melody guitar sold to an online anonymous bidder for ten-thousand-euros, shocking Declan. One of Noah's helmets, from his race win in Monaco, sold for a whopping quarter of a million and it was Noah himself who purchased it, shrugging when Charlie smacked him on the shoulder, the room erupting into laughter when Noah declared it was all grand, after all the kids got their money.

Then it was Emil's jersey up for grabs. Emil had signed it and framed it, along with the captain's armband while also banning Oskar from bidding for it, his friend pushing him toward the stage to hold the framed jersey as the bidding began.

The bidding started at one thousand, with Emil shocked that it kept going up and up, not in the same amount as Noah's helmet, but he was just surprised that any Irish person would want his Danish jersey. Two bidders were fighting hard for the jersey, and the current price was twenty-five thousand.

One of the bidders came back with an offer of twenty-six thousand and the announcer asked if there was anyone who could beat that and the opponents shook their heads and Emil smiled.

"Fifty thousand euros."

Emil snapped his head up at the sound of Luke's voice and drank him in. Dressed in a charcoal grey suit and black shirt, Luke stood at the top of the stairs and he looked gorgeous. His red hair had been styled and his reddish stubble trimmed. He stood at the top of the stairs, those devasting lips of his curving into a smile as the announcer declared the item was sold.

This couldn't be real; this had to be a figment of his imagination. He had to have conjured him up because Emil had truly wanted to see him tonight, even if tomorrow they would go back to pretending they had not shared what they had over the last few months.

Luke started to descend the stairs; flashes of cameras as green eyes held Emil's. There was an intensity in his eyes that Emil had seen before, anytime they had made love and now, he was looking at him with the same intensity and Emil felt his cheeks heat.

Emil saw the flash of uncertainty crossing fleetingly over Luke's features, and then he unbuttoned his jacket, pushed his shoulders back, and the man who held his heart came down the stairs, headed straight for Emil and he forgot how to breathe.

CHAPTER TWENTY-NINE

Luke

LUKE'S calm exterior betrayed the way his heart raced from the moment he opened his mouth and bid for Emil's jersey. He had the winning bid and now, now he was gonna try and win the heart of the man he loved. It was the most nerve-wracking moment of his life but Emil was worth it.

As Luke descended the stairs, the ballroom, one that had fallen into silence at his arrival, now all stood and started to clap for him. Most of the Rebel Racers team had not seen him since the crash and he could see the emotion in their eyes.

But Luke only wanted to focus on one person right now.

Emil looked stunned to see him even as Luke walked through the ballroom to the stage where he jogged up the steps and posed for a picture as Emil handed him over the jersey. Luke set the jersey down and leaned it against the wall, then straightened, knowing that these next few moments would decide how the rest of his life would pan out.

"What are you doing here?" Emil asked him, his tone husky.

Luke turned to face him, his heart pounding, knowing that there were cameras watching the interaction with eager eyes. Right about now, the article Andi had set up for him would be going out in the world, had wanted to prove to Emil that he was not ashamed to be seen with him or to show the world just how much he loved Emil.

He was done hiding and Emil had helped him find the courage to be brave.

Luke took a step closer, Emil's eyes widening as he quickly glanced over his shoulder and back to Luke as Luke grinned. "I've come to show the world who I am. I've come to tell you that I love you and I'm ready to prove it."

Not giving Emil a chance to react, Luke grabbed the lapels of Emil's suit and pulled him closer, crushing his lips to Emil's, losing himself in this, the most important of kisses. Luke drowned out the shocked gasps, the wolf whistles, and just poured his emotions into the kiss to try and convince Emil that they could have something special.

Luke broke the kiss, letting go of Emil's suit, both of them were breathing hard but Emil's eyes were wide. "What have you done?"

Luke heard a murmur in the crowd and knew that the article had gone live so Luke reached out and took Emil's hands in his. "Right now, the world is getting to know the real me. But you knew who I was all along. You saw me when I didn't see myself. I thought long and hard about a lot of things after you left and do you know what I realized?"

Emil interlocked his fingers with Luke, relief surging through him as he continued. "Formula one was lost to me. I can't race because it could kill me. I accepted it. I did. When I asked myself if I could survive without being a racer, I knew the answer was yes. And yet, when I asked myself if I could survive without you, my heart knew that I couldn't."

"Luke," Emil said his name, filled with emotion.

"I came here tonight, to stand in front of everyone, a gay man, who is in love with a gorgeous man in body and soul. I know it won't be easy, I might revert to form, but I want it all with you, Emil. When I look to the future, it's all uncertain at the moment. But the one thing that is crystal clear is that when I look to the future, I'm standing beside you."

Emil took Luke's face in his hands and pressed his

lips quickly to his. "Are you sure? Are you sure this is what you want?"

"I've never been surer that I want you."

Emil didn't say anything for a moment, and for one horrifying second, Luke considered that Emil might not want him anymore, that the intimacy they shared between them had vanished the moment the real world had come down on them.

Luke could feel his cheeks heat, and he took a step back, acutely aware that everyone was watching them. Emil didn't say anything, despite the fact that he still held Luke's hand. He tried to pull his hands back, but Emil held them firmly.

"Would you dance with me?" Emil asked him and Luke almost sagged in relief.

"Absolutely, I will."

Luke blocked out the crowd as they stepped down off the stage and someone must have gotten some music going because other couples had gathered on the dancefloor. Emil led him into the centre of the floor and they were surrounded by all their friends.

Having never danced with a man before, Luke wasn't sure how to do it, and when he looked confused, Emil chuckled, taking Luke's hands and putting them on his slender hips. Then Emil placed his hands on the side of Luke's neck and they swayed, and Luke felt like he could take on the world, with Emil by his side.

"I cannot believe you made all that spectacle for

me. And I cannot believe how much you paid for the jersey. Please tell me you didn't sell a kidney to purchase it."

Luke chuckled, winking at Emil. "No. I did sell the Ferrari though. "

Emil stumbled over his feet and glared at Luke. "What possessed you to do that?"

Luke shrugged, leaning his forehead against Emil's, a flash of a camera as a photographer took their picture. "I didn't think a Ferrari would be the most practical in the Danish winters."

Emil's jaw dropped and Luke made the most of the opportunity, swooping in to steal a kiss that had his own cock hardening and from the hard rigidness of Emil's own cock against him.

When they broke apart, Emil's lips were kiss swollen, and red. "You want to come to Denmark with me?"

"I would go anywhere with you, Emil. Anywhere."

Emil blinked his eyes, dark eyes under even darker lashes, stared at him intently. "I feel like this is a dream. But I never did tell you..." Emil's voice trailed off his hands falling from Luke's neck as he glanced away shyly, but Luke slid his hands up to cup Emil's face.

"Never told me what?" Luke asked as he kept expecting the ball to drop and Emil to realize that Emil was far too good for him.

"That I love you."

Luke's heart felt like it was fit to burst as he

grinned, stealing a quick kiss before he said. "I love you too."

They kissed a little more, Luke soon forgetting that he had just come out to the world and jumping head-first into a relationship. He forgot how scared he had been, formulating his plan with Charlie, Noah, and Andi, and just focused on the man kissing him.

Luke felt a bump to his shoulder, dragging his lips from Emil's as Luke dropped his hands and looked to see Quinn dancing beside them with Oskar, the biggest grin on her face.

"You two seriously need to get a room."

Emil chuckled, placing a hand on Luke's chest. "Oh, we plan to darling. We definitely plan to."

Luke blushed, heat flushing his face as everyone laughed. There was a heated stare on him, Luke letting his eyes drift to where Oskar was looking at him. The other Danish man inclined his head, the unspoken words clear in his expression; that Emil was important to him and they would have serious words if Luke hurt him.

Not that Luke blamed him, as if he had been awake when Oskar and Quinn had started, Luke would have had the same kind of conversation with Oskar about Quinn.

Luke was amazed at how easy their relationship and Luke's coming out had been received among the Rebel Racers, and the night had been absolutely amaz-ing. Luke had laughed, and danced, and thoroughly enjoyed himself, and when the night ended, in the early hours of the morning, and Luke and Emil had returned to Emil's hotel, there had been a laziness to their lovemaking, like they had all the time in the world.

After, as Emil lay on his side, dancing his fingers along Luke's chest, Luke knew that there was no point in wishing that the crash had never happened because if it hadn't then perhaps it would have been an age before Luke and Emil crossed paths, and never gotten together.

Emil rolled on top of Luke, bringing their bodies closer to one another, a devilish grin on his lips as he rocked his hips and Luke sucked in a breath. "Again?"

Luke's lover reached between their bodies, sliding a hand up and down Luke's shaft and Luke threw back his head and moaned, wondering if this heat, this chemistry between them would ever fade as Emil kissed Luke's neck, his collarbone, before trailing his hot, wet, lips down his sternum and before Luke's mind went completely to mush, he certainly hoped not.

CHAPTER THIRTY

Luke

***ONE MONTH** later*

Luke had been prepared for the media storm after he had so publicly come out, and with Emil also being so high profile, and yet, he hadn't been prepared to be inundated with interview requests, and endorsements, and had even been asked to appear on TV as a commentator when the F1 season restarted.

All of that had come as a shock. Luke had taken some time to consider his options on where his new non-driver life would begin, but he was concentrating on getting to know more about Emil. They had taken a week-long trip to Denmark where Emil had introduced Luke to his sisters and his mother, and shown him around the little fishing village where Emil and Oskar had grown up.

Then Emil had spent a few days with Luke's family and Luke had just laughed when Mick had tossed a tea towel at Luke and told him to get drying some glasses while he showed Emil how to pull a proper pint. Luna and the band had stopped by for a few drinks, Luna taking Emil aside and after what looked like an intense conversation, Luna had thrown her arms around Emil, kissing his cheek.

The first few days had been a massive adjustment for Luke, but he had been open and honest with Emil any time that he had felt his fears threatened to undo him. Emil made it easy for him, even taking Luke's lead and doing what Luke felt comfortable in, his boyfriend understanding that Luke was trying.

Boyfriend. Hearing that word made him smile.

Last night they had gone for dinner with Oskar and Quinn, and Noah and Charlie, the restaurant filled to the brim with people, some starstruck and staring at the celebrities in their mists. Emil had sat next to Luke, his arm clung around the back of Luke's seat, and every now and then, the ghost of a touch on Luke's back to reassure him.

It was a lovely evening and the first time that Luke had been out to dinner as part of a couple group. When Luke said to the rest of the group that he felt rather grown up, having a civilized dinner, everyone had laughed.

Noah had cornered him after the meal, asking him to come by the race track tomorrow because he wanted to talk to him about something. Charlie had indicated that since all the family was well now, referring to Luke, that Noah was keen on setting a date for the wedding, with Noah saying that he had to get the ring on Charlie's finger in case she saw sense and tried to run.

Luke assumed Noah was going to ask him to be part of his wedding party. He was nervous to go to the track, not sure how he would feel now that he was retired. Emil had come with him, his support unwavering. When they arrived at the track, Luke could hear the unmistakable sound of an engine roaring as they got out of the car.

Emil took his hand as they walked around the main building, Luke was not sure why Noah would call him here if someone was having a private track day. But it wasn't an F1 car that whizzed past them as they rounded the corner.

What looked like a rally car was booting it around the track, drifting around the corners in a way Luke had always admired, even trying to emulate it when he and Noah had done a track day once in a similar car. Luke couldn't see who was driving the car. However, it wasn't Noah, who was standing just outside the entrance to one of the garages with his arms folded across his chest.

Noah turned his head in their direction, and called

Luke over, Emil squeezing his hand before he perched himself on a low wall and left Luke to go and speak with his friend. Luke strode over and stood next to Noah.

The driver in the car flew around the corner, his tyres screeching as they drifted, the back of the car kicking out before the driver wrangled control of it and flew across the line.

"You fancy having a go?"

Luke slid his gaze to Noah, who wasn't looking at him at all, so missed the dark look Luke was throwing at him. "In case you forgot, I can never race again."

"From what I hear, you can't race in F1 again. So I did a little digging."

Luke was terrified to think too much about Noah's words, to let the little spark of hope kindle in his chest only to be disappointed.

"So, I spoke with your doctors and while you can't race in F1 again, they said there was nothing stopping you from driving in other motorsports."

Luke ran his hands through his hair. "Noah, they told me I couldn't."

"Bullshit," Noah said as he turned to look at Luke. "I spent the last few weeks talking to doctors and specialists who looked at your scans and all super smart shit that I didn't understand. The chances of you damaging your hip again if you drove a rally car is statistically less than in an F1 car. The rollbars, the seats, everything in the car can be tailored to you as a driver and limit the damage if you did have a crash."

Luke looked over at the rally car that had pulled in off to the side, the door opening and a driver got out, Luke sucking in a breath when the driver stood upright, removed his helmet, and grinned like an idiot. It was probably rude, but Luke's eyes immediately went to the prosthesis of the driver's right leg.

"That's Jack O'Neill. You might remember that he was one of the young karters Philip was interested in signing. He was involved in a crash with his family and lost his right leg from the knee down. I've just offered Jack a contract to race for our new team and I want you to drive too."

Luke didn't know what to say as the young man saluted at them and Noah pointed to the car. "It's something that I've wanted to do for a while, invest money in other sports and give people a chance to race when F1 isn't possible. Jack has what it takes to drive and win races. So do you. We can adapt the cars to your liking and you'll have to find a navigator, but what do you say?"

It was on the tip of his tongue to say yes, to jump in with both feet but Luke wasn't sure he wanted to spend all his time driving a car and away from Emil. Luke glanced over his shoulder, then back at Noah, blushing when Noah grinned.

"I'd be the same if I was leaving Charlie at home for months at a time. But as far as I know, I've heard that quite a few races would be taking place in Ireland, England, and Denmark." Luke grinned back at Noah, listening as Noah went on. "I've put my own money in and so has Quinn, but we want you to invest in the team and drive as well. This will be ours, yours, mine, and Quinn's. and if you don't like the name, we can have a board meeting over drinks and decide on it."

Luke looked over at the car, and saw the bright red lettering on the side: NLQ Racing – Noah Luke Quinn racing.

"You have a second chance to have it all, Luke. You can have the boyfriend. You can have the career. It might not have been the career that you dreamed of but you can still be a world champion. It's still a car at the end of the day. You can still show them all what you can do. So how about it, are you in?"

Emil had come over to stand with them then, having heard the last few sentences Noah had spoken. Luke glanced at Emil, the decision not just Luke's anymore as the corners of Emil's mouth turned up into a smile. "I quite fancy being a rally driver's boyfriend."

With Emil's blessing, Luke looked into Noah's grey eyes. "And you're sure that the doctors said I could race. I can't get excited and lose it all again. I can't."

"We can talk to the doctors again but I made sure, Luke. I wouldn't do it to you. Come on, what do you say?"

Luke pouched on Noah, embracing his friend, Noah clapping him on the back. He let Noah go to kiss Emil, wondering how in the hell he got so lucky? Life might have thrown everything at him, but today he stood on his own two feet, being his true self, having the love of a great man, a family he could count on through thick and thin, and now, thanks to Noah, a new lease on life and a new passion to dive into.

There was nothing holding him back now, nothing to hide.

The road might have been bumpy, full of twists and turns and hardships, but in the end, Luke had found love when all hope was lost and he would grab hold of life with both hands, and never lose sight of what was important to him ever again.

THE END

The Rebel County Universe Stories continue in
Make Or Break (Rebel Rock Book 3)

Find More Rebel Stories On Kindle Vella

Crash and Burn is the third novel in the Rebel Racers Trilogy. Rebel Racers is part of the Rebel County Universe which will span at least four different businesses, with intersecting timelines, and characters popping up when you least expect them.

The Rebel Racers Trilogy
Available Now:
Adrenaline Junkie (Rebel Racers Book 1)
All or Nothing (Rebel Racers Book 2)
Crash And Burn (Rebel Racers Book 3)

The Rebel Rock Trilogy
Available Now:
Centre Stage (Rebel Rock Book 1)
Strings Attached (Rebel Rock Book 2)

Susan Harris

Make Or Break (Rebel Rock Book 3)

Coming Soon:
Rebel Ink Trilogy
Rebel Books Trilogy

Playlists

Luke

3 Doors Down - Kryptonite

Remy Zero - Save Me

Bring Me The Horizon - Avalanche

Limp Bizkit - Break Stuff

Architects - Animals

Des Rocs - Hanging by a Thread

Hot Milk - I Think I Hate Myself

IDLES - Car Crash

Beartooth - Skin

Nothing But Thieves - Soda

NF - Paralyzed

NF - Leave Me Alone

Nothing But Thieves - Broken Machine

YONAKA - Waves

Chase & Status - All Goes Wrong

Emil

Imagine Dragons – Natural

YONAKA - Punch Bag

Nina Nesbitt - Summer Fling - GBX & Sparkos Mix

Yuma X - Secret Lover

The National - Sorrow

Goodboys - Black & Blue

Biscits - Let You Go

Felix Jaehn - Rain In Ibiza

Sigrid - Bad Life

Nothing But Thieves - Painkiller

Maggie Lindemann - how could you do this to me? feat. Kellin Quinn from Sleeping With Sirens

You Me At Six - Loverboy - Alternative Mix

Ruelle - In It

Keir - Shiver - Acoustic Session

Pete Tong - You Got The Love (feat. Jules Buckley & The Heritage Orchestra) - Tiësto Remix

ACKNOWLEDGMENTS

***None of this would be possible without an
amazing team supporting me! Many thanks to:***

Publishing House: CTP Publishing
Cover design: Gem Promotions
Interior Formating: Gem Promotions

———

And as always:

Thank you to all the readers!
Whether this is your first book by me or you've been
with me for years! I only get to do this because of you,
and I am eternally grateful to each and every one of
you who took a chance on this Irish author.

About the Author

Susan Harris is a writer from Cork, Ireland and when she's not torturing her readers with heart-wrenching plot twists or killer cliffhangers, she's probably getting some new book related ink, binging her latest TV or music obsession, or with her nose in a book.

Susan LOVES connecting with her fans!
www.susanharrisauthor.com

Also by Susan Harris

The Ever Chace Chronicles

Skin & Bones, book 1

Collateral Damage, book 2

Smoke & Mirrors, book 3

Night of the Hunter, book 4

Never Back Down, book 5

Shortcut to the Grave, book 6

Arsonist's Lullaby, book 7

Of Gods & Monsters, book 8

———

Defy The Stars

A Tale of Two Houses, book 1

Until Death Do Us Part, book 2

In Defiance of the Stars, book 3

Courting Darkness (A Defy The Stars Novella)

———

SHATTERED MEMORIES

———

THE SANGUINE CROWN

Chaos Theory, book 1

Butterfly Effect, book 2

Wicked Game, book 3

Burn Notice, book 4

Fight Song, book 5

THE SICARIUS SECURITY SERIES

Kiss Of Death, book 1

Leap Of Faith, book 2

Visions Of Destiny, book 3

War of Hearts, book 4